The Little Jasoos &

Other Stories

RAM K. BHATTACHARYA

INDIA · SINGAPORE · MALAYSIA

Notion Press

Old No. 38, New No. 6
McNichols Road, Chetpet
Chennai - 600 031

First Published by Notion Press 2019
Copyright © Ram K. Bhattacharya 2019
All Rights Reserved.

ISBN 978-1-64429-742-1

This book is dedicated to my late father Shri Ram Dulal Bhattacharya who has been my inspiration for everything in my life.

Contents

foreword

Imagine you are an eight-year-old again, and all the little mysteries, vagaries and skirmishes in life loom large as you prepare to navigate your childhood with your sibling. Now imagine being armed with a genuinely curious mind, some very sharp sleuthing skills and a talent for sniffing out situations where you could use these skills. If you end up helping other kids and adults, you're all the happier for it.

I have just described Tejas and Shreyas, the main protagonists of "The Little Jasoos". I have modelled them after the adventures of my own grandsons, who have delighted me for years with their various escapades.

I am a retired Executive Director of BHEL. Since my retirement, I have dabbled in food & travel writing on social media and fiction-writing in both Bengali and English. I now have the luxury of time with my grandsons, who delight me with their stories as often as I delight them with mine, and who have really been the inspiration behind my protagonists.

I am excited at the thought of sharing these stories, so they may be enjoyed by other children as well. I am sure even adults would find these little escapades by the young children very interesting and refreshing.

I would like to express special thanks to my family, who have been both my inspiration and backbone through this entire process. My wife Krishna has always been my rock, providing immense moral support, and a 'patient ear' to hear my stories. My daughters, Aparajita and Kamalika, and sons, Ajay and Arijit, have put in long hours of effort to edit and work with the publishers to make this book what it is. Special thanks to Arijit and Kirti, who let their creative energies flow to create the beautiful illustrations you see in the book. I am blessed to have such a supportive family.

Lastly, I am thankful to my close friend Dr. Santanu Dasgupta for putting the idea of starting on a children's book into my head to set the ball rolling.

– Ram Kamal Bhattacharya

Introduction

Tejas and Shreyas are two young brothers, eight and six, growing up in exciting modern-day Bengaluru city, with the customary set of working parents and doting grandparents. While they have all the normal interests, like Cricket and Football, Tejas and Shreyas share a love for detecting. They don't always understand the world of adults and some of their actions seem rather funny, but that does not discourage the analytical and thorough Tejas as he applies his logical mind to problems, with his much more people-oriented brother Shreyas, helping him navigate the world.

Living in a large apartment complex, they come across different characters in their everyday life in the middle of school, summer camp, summers with grandparents etc. Each of these characters has a problem or a situation in which they find themselves. Together, the brothers detect, mull over plans at night in bed and put their plans into action, helping other children and sometimes, even adults, get themselves out of scrapes and skirmishes, often with hilarious results. Everyone around them is amazed at the inventiveness of these little children, and help in any way they can, whether it is Baba giving the right explanations, or their sometimes detecting partner Mohinder Uncle, or even their own Dadu. From helping a child being bullied to recovering a lost water bottle, Tejas and Shreyas are the little detectives, who are forever ready to help anyone in trouble.

The Little Jasoos is a collection of ten short stories of the adventures of Tejas and Shreyas.

1. The Little Jasoos

The Worried Lady

Mamtaji had come to visit *Ajji* (grandmother) in the evening. Whenever they were together, they spent many hours talking about a whole variety of topics. Now dusk had fallen and it was time for *Mamtaji* to go home. She stood up to gather her things and leave.

Ajji also got up and asked her friend a question – "So, how is *Keshavji?*" *Keshavji* was *Mamtaji's* husband and was in his mid-sixties. "Oh, he is mostly alright – but for the last month he has been suffering from very severe stomach upsets."

"It must be the food, make sure he takes only non-spicy home-made food." – said *Ajji*.

Mamtaji had stopped on the way to the door. Now she turned around and faced *Ajji* – "That's what I do. I am the only one who cooks his meals. I cook his vegetables with very little oil and add only a small amount of spices. No,

I don't think there is any problem with the home food."

Ajji asked – "Does he eat outside food often?"

Mamtaji shook her head – "No, we hardly ever eat any. But there is one thing – he is very fond of *chatpata* snacks. I don't know whether he eats them without my knowledge."

"Have you ever asked him if he does?" – asked *Ajji*.

Mamtaji was almost at the door and said – "Yes, but he says he knows how to take care of his health, so I guess he tries to avoid answering that question. If I persist, he gets angry." With a parting smile, *Mamtaji* left waving goodbye to her friend and the kids.

The Compassionate Kids

The two children in the house, Tejas and Shreyas Joshi were quietly sitting in the drawing room minding their own business while the two ladies were talking. They also liked *Mamtaji* as she would always speak a few words with the children first and would always bring some home-made snacks for them. Today she had brought *laddus* for them.

Tejas at seven and a half was very fond of reading books and was deeply immersed today in the latest 'Famous Five' book that his father had bought for him. It was a gift to reward Tejas for his silver medal in the School Athletics Competition.

The five-year old Shreyas was more eager to do drawing and painting. His current favourite was Lord Hanuman and he was trying to draw the latest 'Avatar' of Hanuman as a musician. All through the conversation, he was deeply absorbed in his drawing.

The two young boys were very different in nature. While Tejas would be deeply absorbed in reading and would not pay much attention to what was happening or was being said around him, Shreyas would hear and know all that was going on nearby, despite being absorbed in his task. Therefore, while Tejas did not hear the conversation between *Ajji* and *Mamtaji*, Shreyas had heard everything, which got him interested and set him thinking.

After *Mamtaji* left, *Ajji* shut the door and went to her room to do some 'Yogasana' before dinner. Shreyas put the last touches on his Hanuman playing a 'Dholak' and walked over to where Tejas was still absorbed in his book. Softly he asked – "*Dada*, may I disturb you a little?"

Tejas lifted his hand and said – "Wait for just one minute." He was very precise in his statements, one minute would mean exactly one minute. Shreyas waited patiently. He knew that *Dada* became very angry if disturbed, especially when he was at an interesting part of his book.

Tejas finished what he was reading, closed the book and looked at Shreyas – "Yes, Shreyas, what is it? You look like you're up to something."

Shreyas said with a serious face – "*Mamta ajji* came, you know?"

Tejas was annoyed at being disturbed while reading, for such a small thing, and in an irritated tone, said – "Yes, I know that. Now what is it you wanted to ask or tell me?"

Shreyas's face remained serious – "You know her husband Keshav Uncle is not well!"

Tejas was still annoyed – "OK, but what can a small kid like me do? He should go to a Doctor."

Shreyas said – "Yes, he can, but we have to find out why he is getting sick and try to prevent that in future."

Tejas was losing his patience – "But what can you and I do? The people in their house should take care of him."

4

Shreyas was a little hurt at Tejas's words. He said in a slightly choked voice –"But *Dada*, *Mamta-ajji* is our *Ajji's* best friend and she brings so many things for us. She is worried for him. Should we not try to help her at all?"

Tejas's heart softened noting Shreyas's sincere distress at seeing *Mamtaji's* worry for her husband. He put his hand on Shreyas's shoulder and said – "Ok, Shreyas. First tell me the whole story."

Shreyas repeated the conversation between *Mamtaji* and *Ajji*, regarding *Keshavji's* health and added at the end – "This is all that I heard. I have a feeling Keshav Uncle eats some unhealthy food outside without letting anybody know. *Mamta-ajji* said he was very fond of *chatpata* food."

Tejas was excellent in logical thinking – he had always been able to connect events with clear reasons. He now started thinking about all that Shreyas had told him. His face remained serious and realizing that *Dada* was thinking, Shreyas also kept quiet.

After a couple of minutes, Tejas said – "Shreyas, we have to find out all that Keshav Uncle does when he is not in the house."

Shreyas asked – "But how?"

Tejas put his fingers on his lips – "Let's not talk about it now. We should not let *Baba*,

Mamma and *Ajji* know what we are doing. They may tell us not to bother about it. Let's talk again tonight when we go to our room to sleep, okay?"

Shreyas nodded and the two trooped out of the living room to help their *Mamma* set the dining table for dinner.

Planning in Progress

After dinner that night and spending some time in front of the TV, *Mamma* said – "Come on kids, let me put you to sleep. You have to get up early tomorrow for school."

Both of them said in unison – "*Mamma*, we shall go to sleep by ourselves, you don't have to come. Please make the bed for us."

Mamma said with doubt in her voice – "But will you? Every night you two start fighting and jumping on the bed if I am not around and don't sleep until it is very late."

"No Mamma, we promise we won't fight tonight."

Mamma was secretly pleased. At last the boys were learning how to behave! She said – "Okay, my good boys! Good night."

Both chorused – "Good night, *Mamma*. Please turn off the light and close the door."

As *Mamma* switched off the light, closed the door and left, the brothers waited for a few minutes to make sure that she was really gone, before continuing their conversation from earlier in the day. Shreyas, not wanting to take any chances on being caught, said – "*Dada*, let's speak softly so that *Baba* and *Mamma* cannot hear us, okay?"

Tejas said – "OK, so let's plan things. The idea is to watch Keshav Uncle."

Shreyas said – "But *Dada*, the whole day we are in school. How can we watch him all the time?"

Tejas said – "Try to look at it logically, Shreyas. The daytime is very hot and sunny and an old man like Keshav Uncle will not like to go out then. It will be very uncomfortable for him."

Shreyas agreed – "Yes that is true. But what does that mean for the plan?"

Tejas continued – "That means he comes out only after five O'clock when it is not so hot, and that is exactly when we also go downstairs to play."

Shreyas suddenly remembered something – "You are right! I have seen him sitting on a bench near where we play football."

Tejas said – "So the plan is to keep watching him, as he sits on the bench, while we play."

Shreyas was excited and said loudly – "*Dada*, then we can follow him to see where he goes, whenever he gets up from his bench."

Tejas said– "Shhh! Do you want *Mamma* and *Baba* to catch us talking? Keep your voice down. But you have got it. Whatever Keshav Uncle eats outside, he must be doing so between the time he comes down to sit on the bench and when he goes back home before dark."

Shreyas asked – "But after we find out, what do we do?"

By now, Tejas was sleepy and said – "Let's find out first. Then we shall see what to do."

The boys went to sleep feeling satisfied that they had a plan to catch Keshav Uncle in the act.

The Little Jasoos in Action

Tejas and Shreyas started their watching game from the next day. They did not tell their playmates anything about the plan.

Keshav Uncle was not to be seen for the first two days. Perhaps he was too unwell to come down for his evening walk.

He came down the next two days, but sat and watched the children play and did not go out of the Apartment Complex. Then on the fifth day, the boys met with success in their detecting.

Since it was still summer, it was still quite uncomfortable at five O'clock when Tejas, Shreyas and their friends started playing football. Since both Tejas and Shreyas were attending Soccer Camp during the weekends, they were the star players in their group. That evening, the play started as usual and Tejas and Shreyas were playing with great enthusiasm. Even while playing, they kept a watch on the bench where Keshav Uncle usually came and sat. But today, he had not yet come, maybe to avoid the heat.

Finally at five-thirty, Keshav Uncle came and sat on the bench, lazily watching the children's game, though his mind seemed somewhere else. Without his knowledge, the Joshi boys were observing all of this.

After about half an hour, Keshav Uncle got up and started walking towards the exit gate of the Complex. Previously for the last two days, he had always got up, only to head back home. The boys immediately saw an opportunity to catch Keshav Uncle in the act of whatever was causing *Mamta-ajji* so much worry. Tejas and Shreyas exchanged glances and started walking in the same direction as Keshav Uncle, leaving the game behind.

Tejas's friend Rajesh shouted – "Tejas, where are you going? We are not done with the game yet."

Shreyas quickly thought on his feet and said – "We have to buy something urgently from the shop. We had forgotten about it. We shall play again tomorrow."

Rajesh shouted again – "But, what's the hurry? You can always buy it later, when we finish playing." But by the time he had finished saying this, the two boys had already vanished. Shaking his head at his friend's antics, Rajesh turned back to the game.

Meanwhile, Keshav Uncle walked out of the compound gate and started walking along the road, the boys following at a short distance behind him.

Shreyas asked – "But *Dada*, if Keshav Uncle goes a long distance, how can we follow him? *Baba* will scold us if he comes to know that we were going so far outside by ourselves."

Tejas said – "Don't worry. Keshav Uncle is old – he will not go far."

Tejas was right! *Keshavji* stopped at the Fast Food Centre at the corner not far from the exit gate. The boys stopped a little distance away and kept watch from behind a parked car.

Keshavji looked into the shop to make sure that nobody he knew was there. Finding no one, he went inside. The boys moved forward to ensure they could keep Keshav Uncle in their sights.

The old man had a plate of *chaat*, and after that, some *pani-puri*. With a look of complete satisfaction, he wiped his hands and lips with his handkerchief, paid for his snacks, and started a leisurely walk back to the compound with an expression of satisfaction on his face.

And so, the mystery was solved! Tejas and Shreyas now knew why Keshav Uncle was having stomach problems. But that still left them with the next part of the problem - they still had to figure out how to prevent him from eating these unhealthy snacks in future. That was their next challenge!

Secret Unravelled, but ...?

That night again, Tejas and Shreyas told *Mamma* to leave them alone in their room at bedtime. *Mamma* was happy - the boys were really growing up!

Lights out and door closed, Shreyas asked – "But *Dada*, what do we do now? Can't we just request him not to eat those junk foods?"

Tejas said in a low tone – "No, Shreyas! Old people are sometimes more childish than us kids. He will not listen to anybody."

Shreyas was sad – "So what was the use of following him? He will keep on doing this and *Mamta-ajji's* problem will not be solved."

Tejas, plotting in his head, said – "Hmm.....if a simple request will not change his habits......"

Shreyas asked – "Then what will, *Dada*?"

Tejas thought quietly for a few moments and then said softly – "I think we have to get him really scared."

Shreyas was curious, and asked – "How do we do that?"

Tejas said in a sleepy tone – "I have no idea, Shreyas. But let me think. You also do some thinking." Then he promptly fell asleep.

Shreyas lay awake for some time, thinking seriously and after a while, a hint of an idea started forming in his mind. Finally the effort was too much – he also fell asleep.

The Idea!

In the usual early morning rush to get ready for school the next morning, Tejas and Shreyas completely forgot about their problem. That day, at school, they were all busy preparing for the upcoming Sports Day and their problem with Keshav Uncle went completely out of their minds. But as soon as they lined up for the school bus at the end of the day, Shreyas remembered the solution he had thought up the night before. He whispered to Tejas, who was standing behind him in line that he needed to speak to him privately.

"*Dada*, I found a solution."

Tejas's mind was still on the activities at school and didn't immediately catch what Shreyas was talking about. "What solution, Shreyas? What are you talking about?"

Shreyas was surprised too, seeing that his elder brother had forgotten all about the problem they were solving together – "What, *Dada*! Have you forgotten about Keshav Uncle?"

Tejas now remembered – "Oh yes, sorry I forgot! What's your solution?"

Shreyas looked around him. They were surrounded by kids who went to their school and were also neighbours – "No, not here! Let's sit in the back row of the bus and talk. Nobody will be able to hear us there."

In the privacy of the back row in the bus, Shreyas told his elder brother about the plan he had hatched the night before. Shreyas's face was glowing with excitement as he outlined his solution.

Tejas was truly surprised – "Brilliant idea, Shreyas! But do you think it will work?"

Shreyas said excitedly – "Yes, it will! It is my idea and I shall make it work."

Tejas nodded and said – "But it will require good acting. Can you act?"

Shreyas said confidently – "You wait and see, *Dada*. I'll be really good at it. But, when do you think we should put it into action?"

Tejas, secretly very proud of his brother, was now sure of the idea and said – "There is no reason to wait. Let's do it today."

The Act and the Result

Like on previous days, Tejas and Shreyas went down to play with their friends at five O'clock, but, unlike other days, did not join the game. Despite their friends' constant urging to join them, they hung around near the bench where Keshav Uncle usually sat. They chose a place where the old man would not notice them, but they could see him. At around five-thirty, *Keshavji* came and sat down on the usual bench.

The boys now made their move.

Walking back a few paces from where they were waiting, they stopped for a few seconds like sprinters do at the start of a race. Then they took off running in a similar manner.

Shreyas started howling and crying, while running towards the bench where *Keshavji* was sitting. Tejas closely followed him urging him not to cry. Dramatically, Shreyas stopped right in front of *Keshavji*, but continued crying. Tejas soon joined him, still trying to console him and urging him to stop crying.

Surprised to see Shreyas crying, *Keshavji* (who obviously knew the boys as *Ajji's* grandkids) was all concern "What happened, Shreyas? Why are you crying?"

Shreyas did not answer but continued crying.

Keshavji then asked Tejas – "Tejas! Have you done something to Shreyas? Why is he crying?"

Tejas protested – "I didn't do anything, Uncle. Shreyas, why don't you stop crying and tell Uncle what happened?"

Shreyas now stopped crying and wiped his eyes and said –"Uncle, three of my friends Naveen, Akshath and Adil are very sick in the hospital."

Keshavji was shocked – "Why?"

Shreyas spoke in a choked voice – "They ate *pani-puri* and *chaat* yesterday from the fast food shop at the corner. They've been complaining of a lot of stomach pain and diarrhoea since then."

Tejas chipped in – "Food poisoning – it looks like."

Shreyas continued – "My friends' parents are very upset and have been shouting at that uncle in the shop. They are talking about calling the police."

Keshavji's face suddenly went pale and unknowingly, his hands went to his stomach. Telling the boys to go home, he hastily got up and started walking rapidly towards his building.

When *Keshavji's* figure was no longer visible, Tejas and Shreyas broke into a wide smile and did a 'High Five' enthusiastically.

The Relieved Lady

Mamtaji visited *Ajji* again after fifteen days at her usual time in the evening. Tejas and Shreyas were busy in the living room doing their homework.

After some casual conversation, *Ajji* raised the topic –"How is *Keshavji's* health now? Did you take him to a Doctor?"

Mamtaji's face lit up "He does not like going to a Doctor, but he is fine now. I don't know what happened, but no upset stomachs for the last ten days."

Ajji said –"How did it get cured, Mamtaji? Please tell me, I may also need the trick sometime!"

–"No idea, but whatever it was, it has done him a lot of good. Let's thank God for whatever it was."

Unnoticed by the ladies, the 'Gods' exchanged glances with a faint smile.

After *Mamtaji's* departure, as *Ajji* closed the door and came back into the living room, she saw the two boys doing a 'High Five' in the middle of the room with big smiles on their faces.

She was puzzled, but did not ask the reason. She just smiled and went into her room.

2. Swachh Bharat

Appeal of the Message

Tejas and Shreyas's father was watching the news on the television in the evening. The Newsreader was talking about the good things being done by the new government. Shortly, she came to the subject of 'Swachh Bharat'. As the news item was being read, a nice song accompanied the TV broadcast.

Shreyas was piecing together a difficult jig-saw puzzle of 300 pieces. He had been allowed to play as he had finished his homework earlier in the evening. Tejas was reading a book in one corner of the room. He always liked to concentrate fully on his reading and did not like it when anyone disturbed him while reading. He too had finished his homework earlier. The parents were glad that the kids had found better ways to spend their time at home rather than watching TV.

The two boys were quite different in nature. The seven-and-a-half year-old Tejas

Joshi was more driven by logic and reason whereas the five-year-old Shreyas Joshi went more by his feelings and emotions for others. So, for the same message given to both, Tejas would look at the substance of the sentence, but Shreyas would try to think about the meaning and spirit behind it.

The nice song, as well as the manner in which the Newsreader announced the term 'Swachh Bharat', suddenly caught Shreyas's attention. He asked his elder brother – "Dada, what is 'Swachh Bharat'?"

Tejas lifted his face from his book for a second and said – "I don't know, ask Baba." He went back to his reading.

Shreyas knew it was not proper to disturb Baba when he was listening to the news. As soon as it was over and Baba switched off the TV, Shreyas went to him and asked – "Baba, what is 'Swachh Bharat'?"

Baba liked the kids wanting to know about things outside their studies and he was always very patient in explaining things. He said – "'Swachh' is the Sanskrit word for 'Clean' and 'Bharat' is the Sanskrit name of our country. In other words, 'Swachh Bharat' stands for 'Clean India'. Did you understand?"

Shreyas asked – "But what is Sanskrit?" Obviously, he had not come across this term before.

Baba again said patiently – "Sanskrit is the oldest language of our country and is the mother of all our presently used languages like Hindi, Marathi, Kannada, Bengali, Telugu etc."

Shreyas continued with his question – "But who speaks Sanskrit? I have not heard anybody speaking in that language. Is it what Mani Uncle speaks?" (Mani was the family chauffeur).

Baba laughed with amusement and said – "No Shreyas, Mani speaks Tamil – perhaps the only Indian language not having a major connection with Sanskrit. But do you want to know who still uses Sanskrit in their day-to-day lives?" At Shreyas's nod, he continued "During a *puja*, all the priests chant their '*Mantras*' in Sanskrit. So, you must have heard Sanskrit many times, right?"

Shreyas nodded but was not finished with his questioning – "But what was that Aunty saying about '*Swachh Bharat*'?"

Baba laughingly ruffled Shreyas's short hair – "Our Government wants to make our country clean and wants all of us to do our part in maintaining cleanliness."

By this time, overhearing the conversation Tejas had also joined them and asked – "But *Baba*, we are small children. What can we do for '*Swachh Bharat*'?"

Baba said – "Cleanliness can start from you. First of all, keep your hands, feet, nose, and hair – everything on your body clean. Wear clean clothes and clean shoes. Then keep your room clean, eat your food cleanly without dirtying the dining table and don't dirty your surroundings. Don't throw any paper, plastic bags or food on the road – always throw them in the dustbin. Remember, any unclean person from a dirty household cannot make the surroundings clean."

Shreyas said – "Yes, *Baba*. We do all of this. What else can we do?"

Baba said – "You can tell the people you meet to do the same. It may be a good idea to set an example by picking up trash thrown by irresponsible people."

Tejas said – "If we do that, others also will do the same and our area will be clean. Seeing us small children doing it will put shame on those who had thrown trash, isn't it, *Baba*?"

Baba was glad that the boys were attentive to good lessons. He smiled and said– "Yes, that's right. We all must contribute even if it is in a small way."

Shreyas brightened up and said – "*Baba*, like that little squirrel who helped *Lord Rama* build a bridge to *Ravana's* Lanka, right?"

Baba was genuinely surprised to see the younger one's ability to connect things so perfectly at such a young age. Smiling, he said – "Correct Shreyas! Now let's go and do our bit at present by helping *Mamma* to set the dinner table."

Keeping their conversation with *Baba* in mind, the kids did a splendid job by not dirtying the dining table at all during dinner and taking great care to clean their plates. *Mamma* observed it and felt happy.

Soon it was time for the boys to go to sleep.

Shreyas in Action – Acquires a Friend

The next day was a Saturday and a holiday from school. Shreyas got up early (he was an early riser), but Tejas continued to sleep till later. After brushing his teeth and finishing his business in the bathroom, Shreyas saw that *Ajji* was getting ready to go for her morning walk. Shreyas loved to go for a walk with *Ajji* as the two would talk constantly, Shreyas also would tell *Ajji* Kannada names for many things he learnt from his friends at school. *Ajji* smilingly told Shreyas to put on his shoes and come with her.

As they were about to call for the elevator, Shreyas suddenly remembered something and told his grandmother – "*Ajji*, please open the door for me, I forgot something." *Ajji* complied and Shreyas ran inside and came back with a plastic bag in his hand. *Ajji* was surprised and asked – "Shreyas, what is that bag for?"

Shreyas smiled and said – "*Ajji*, this is for '*Swachh Bharat*'"

Ajji could not connect the bag with the latest buzzword in all media and said – "I don't understand what '*Swachh Bharat*' has got to do with that bag."

Shreyas said a little seriously – "*Ajji*, I want to do my part to make our Complex clean. I have seen many people throwing paper, plastic and other garbage on the road. It looks so dirty. I want to pick them up and put them in the bag."

Ajji asked – "and what will you do with this bag afterwards?"

Shreyas had the answer – "I shall put it in the large dustbin near our building, which is cleaned out by the garbage truck every day."

Ajji was pleasantly surprised to see such good sense in a boy as young as Shreyas and fully supported him in this.

While walking, Shreyas picked up trash from the road thrown by some irresponsible folks. Truly, without the trash, the road looked neat and clean.

Suddenly, Shreyas pulled *Ajji's* hand and said – "*Ajji*, who is that man? Do you know?" He pointed towards an elderly man sitting on the stone bench a little distance away.

Ajji had also seen this man many times in the Complex, but did not know him. The man was tall, lean, very fair and still handsome, despite being well past sixty years of age. He was always very well-dressed. *Ajji* had mostly seen him walking around the Complex during the day and talking sometimes to other people, the Security Staff, the gardeners and to the children while they were playing. He looked very smart and always had a smile on his face. He had one problem though. His upper body (from his waist up) was somewhat stiff and slightly bent at an angle to one side. His neck was also stiff and to look back, he had to turn his whole body around. Shreyas was fascinated by this elderly gentleman and had always wanted to talk to him. *Ajji* said – "I have seen him, but don't know who he is."

Shreyas suddenly said – "Then let's go and talk to him and find out."

Ajji was surprised at Shreyas's sudden interest in this man. Curiously, she followed Shreyas who was now walking rapidly towards him. As he walked up to him, Shreyas addressed him directly – "Good morning, Uncle!"

The man was looking at the screen of his mobile phone and had not noticed Shreyas approaching him. Suddenly he found this little boy standing in front of him and an elderly lady following. With a ready smile, he quickly responded – "Oh, a very good morning to you, son! I am Mohinder and who may you be?"

Shreyas was happy to get this quick and cheerful response from the man he was so fascinated with. He also responded with "I am Shreyas Joshi."

Mohinder shook hands with Shreyas and asked him – "And, how old are you, Shreyas?"

Shreyas said – "I am five years old."

Mohinder asked again – "Which school do you study in and which grade are you in?"

The conversation went on for a minute or so. By that time, *Ajji* had caught up to Shreyas and stood by his side. Seeing her, Mohinder got up and put his palms together in a '*namaste*' to greet *Ajji*. They started to talk, getting acquainted with each other.

In the meantime, Shreyas noticed some chocolate wrappers lying nearby on the ground and picked them up to put them into his bag. Though Mohinder was talking to *Ajji*, he did not fail to notice Shreyas's action and was deeply impressed.

After about five minutes of talking, *Ajji* was ready to continue with her walk. As they were about to leave, Mohinder asked Shreyas – "For what is that bag in your hand, Shreyas?"

Shreyas proudly said – "I am doing my part for '*Swachh Bharat*'. I am picking up the '*Kachra*' (trash) lying on the ground so that the Complex looks clean."

Mohinder was taken aback by the little kid's good sense – "Who asked you to do this?"

Shreyas again proudly said – "Nobody told me, Uncle. They were talking about '*Swachh Bharat*' on TV, and then my *Baba* told me what it means."

Mohinder was by now totally impressed – "You are such a good boy, Shreyas! From tomorrow, we shall do this together, Okay?"

Shreyas instantly beamed from ear to ear "Yes, Uncle."

"So, it's a deal?"

Shreyas responded, happy to have made a friend– "It's a deal." They brought their palms together for a handshake and Shreyas then left with *Ajji* to continue their walk.

As they walked, Shreyas asked his grandmother – "*Ajji*, what was Mohinder Uncle saying to you?"

Ajji said – "He was telling me about himself, just like I was telling him about us." She knew Shreyas's questions would not stop there as he was very curious about people he met.

Shreyas asked – "Would you please tell me as well, *Ajji*?"

Ajji smiled at Shreyas and said – "Ok, why not? Listen now."

Mohinder Taneja was from Kapurthala in Punjab. Having been in the Indian Army for many years, he had retired as a Colonel eleven years back. He was now sixty-five years old. Due to an accident during an Army exercise many years back, he had suffered an injury to his spinal cord, which caused the stiffness in his upper body. He had lost his wife about five years back and was currently staying with his only son Satinder, who lived in the Complex. He had a grandson named Avinash who was about ten years old.

After listening to *Ajji*, Shreyas said – "Yes, I know Avinash. He is a big boy and has many friends. I like him. He always treats us little kids nicely."

After the walk, the duo headed back to the apartment. Shreyas took off his shoes and immediately washed his hands and feet thoroughly. He was happy to be doing his bit for 'Swachh Bharat'. When he told his parents, they were happy too, but *Mamma* cautioned – "Be careful not to pick up dirty things from the road."

Duo Takes Up a Dirty Problem

The very next day Shreyas went down, but with *Baba* this time. He remembered to take a plastic bag for the trash again. Mohinder Uncle's promise of the previous day to work together for 'Swachh Bharat' was very much on his mind. Shreyas was certainly looking forward to seeing him again. Mohinder Uncle seemed to be a very interesting and jovial man and Shreyas felt there was a lot to learn from him.

True to his word, Mohinder Uncle was there in his usual place. As *Baba* and Shreyas approached him, they all greeted one another with 'Good morning'. Shreyas introduced *Baba* and Mohinder Uncle and they talked to each other for a few minutes. Then Mohinder

Uncle said to *Baba* – "Akash, leave Shreyas with me. I promised him yesterday that we would do some good work together. I learnt a very great lesson from Shreyas yesterday. A truly remarkable boy - so different from others of his age!"

Baba felt comfortable with Shreyas being left with Mohinder. He knew Satinder very well and *Ajji* had also mentioned running into Mohinder the day before and the fact that Shreyas and he had become friends. He left Shreyas in Mohinder's capable hands and went on with his morning walk.

Mohinder had brought a *laddu* for Shreyas, his young friend, in a small pouch and gave it to him. Shreyas was delighted and ate the *laddu* sitting next to Mohinder Uncle on the bench and chattering all the time. Once the *laddu* was finished, Mohinder told his little partner – "Shreyas, we have to do something about another dirty problem."

Shreyas was immediately interested – "Uncle, what are you talking about?"

Mohinder said – "Did you notice that some of our fellow-residents in this Complex walk their dogs in the mornings and these dogs are 'pooping' on the road? It is not only dirty, it smells too and after a little while, the flies collect on them."

Shreyas wrinkled his nose in disgust – "Yuck! Some of these flies also try to sit on our face when we come to play. It is so yucky!"

Mohinder smiled seeing Shreyas's uncomfortable expression at the very mention of the subject, as he said – "I know. This has to be prevented."

Shreyas innocently asked – "Could we not simply tell those Uncles not to walk their dogs inside?"

Mohinder said – "Not so simple, Shreyas. These dogs are also living beings and just like us, they have to answer the call of nature. If they are taken outside the gate, the street dogs attack and bite these pet dogs. I have seen a few incidents like this. It is not really safe for the pet dogs or the owners."

Shreyas saw the point and asked – "Then what should be done, Uncle?"

It was clear that Mohinder had given some thought to this problem. He said – "The dog owners can walk their dogs in the Complex as it is safe for their pets. But they have to pick up the poop their dogs leave behind."

Shreyas wrinkled his nose at the very thought of it – "With their hands?"

Mohinder laughed loudly at his little friend's reaction– "No, not with their hands at all. They can get plastic scoops available in the shop. They should come with the scoops and plastic bags in which the 'poops' can be disposed of later in the dustbin."

Shreyas was jubilant – "But how can we tell the Uncles?"

Mohinder shook his head – "That is the difficult part, Shreyas. It is not so easy to change people's behaviour." But he brightened up and said – "I have some idea about how we can do it. Let's go to the Estate Office, and thereafter, to the Security Office."

Shreyas did not know what solution Mohinder Uncle had come up with, but followed him obediently.

As Mohinder talked to the Estate Manager, Manjunath and thereafter to the Security in-charge, Shreyas quietly remained at his side, not entirely following the conversation. But he did pick up some words like 'Notice', 'Scoop', 'Packet' etc. At the end of it as they came out, Shreyas asked – "Mohinder Uncle, now will you please tell me what you talked about in there?"

Mohinder bent down, touched Shreyas on his cheek and said – "You have been very patient, young man. Let's first sit down somewhere. My back is hurting. Then I shall tell you everything."

As they sat down on the stone bench near the play area, Mohinder started speaking. In the meantime, the two of them had visited the store just outside the gate and bought some cakes. Mohinder opened the wrapper, took out two pieces for himself and handed over the rest to Shreyas who accepted it and started eating immediately as he was quite hungry.

Mohinder said – "First, I requested the Estate Manager to issue a notice to all dog owners that we want to keep our Complex clean and that dog owners were requested to bring scoops and plastic bags to remove the dogs' poops. If they cannot do it, the only alternative would be to ask the owners to take their dogs outside the Complex gate for their activities."

Shreyas asked – "But Uncle, how will he know all the people who have dogs in our Complex?"

Mohinder patted Shreyas lightly on his back – "Good question! You see, all dog owners had to register their dogs when they started living in the Complex and even submit a photo of the dog. So, you see, they have a record of all the pet owners in the Complex." Seeing a nod from Shreyas, Mohinder continued, "Secondly, I requested the Security in-charge to tell their Guards to go for a round in the morning to see whether the dog owners are obeying the notice or not. Thirdly, I am going to do something myself."

Shreyas was immediately curious "What, Uncle?"

Mohinder said "I know that the dog owners will not be able to buy the scoop and the plastic bags immediately. It will take them a day or two to get the notice and then go to the shop and buy it. Also, some people may forget to bring them in the morning until it becomes a habit for them. So, I am going to visit the shop today and buy two scoops and some plastic bags. I shall go around myself in the morning when the owners bring their dogs for walking and offer the scoops and the bags to anyone who does not have them. You will have school from Monday to Friday, but can join me on Saturdays and Sundays. I think after the first few days, everybody will learn to do the right thing.

Am I doing it right, Shreyas?" Mohinder Uncle finished with a question to Shreyas smiling.

Shreyas was impressed with Mohinder Uncle's actions and planning. He held Uncle's hand in both of his own and said – "Very right, Uncle. Our Complex will be very clean now."

Mohinder Uncle then said in a very soft tone – "You know Shreyas – I learnt a lot from you yesterday and now nobody can stop me. I am very proud of you. But you have another task to do."

Shreyas asked eagerly – "What task, Uncle?"

Mohinder said – "What you started yesterday should be set as an example to the other boys here. You must talk to all the friends you play football with about what you are trying to do."

Shreyas felt very happy and agreed.

By the time they finished talking, it was time for Shreyas to head back home. Mohinder said – "Come, Shreyas, let me take you home as I had promised your father. From tomorrow, I shall be doing as I told you. But you should also keep your eyes open and keep note of things not being done right. We shall meet again next Saturday morning. Is that okay?"

Shreyas nodded and soon he was deposited back in the Joshi household by his elderly friend.

That evening when the boys got together to play football, Shreyas very confidently explained to the others what 'Swachh Bharat' was, and what he and Mohinder Uncle had started. To his pleasant surprise, everybody agreed to follow the same example.

The Reluctant Fellow and a Lesson

By the next Saturday morning, Shreyas had made some observations and was ready to meet Mohinder Uncle so that they could figure out what to do about the problems he had observed. They met at their usual stone bench.

"Uncle, our Complex looks so clean now! My football friends are also helping. But there is still one problem that I have observed."

Mohinder had stopped being surprised by the capabilities of his little friend a while back. He said – "Good, Shreyas. You have really worked on our mission seriously. Tell me what you have seen."

Shreyas said – "Now all the uncles with dogs are carrying the scoop and bag except one person. He mostly walks his dog in the basement parking area and I have seen the dog's poop lying around there."

Mohinder's eyes became serious – "Do you know who he is, Shreyas?"

Shreyas nodded – "Yes, I know him by sight, but I don't know his name. He lives in our building and I know his house."

Mohinder asked again – "Are you quite sure that the poop you have seen are done by that uncle's dog, Shreyas?"

Shreyas said – "Yes Uncle. No other dog goes into the basement and I have seen that this dog's owner does not carry a scoop."

Mohinder's handsome face became dark. Obviously, he was angry. Gravely he asked – "Shreyas, what can we do to teach him a lesson?"

Shreyas thought for some time and suddenly a brilliant idea popped into his mind. He spoke hurriedly – "Uncle, if he does not want to pick up the poop, we can pick it up and present it to him."

Mohinder was puzzled and asked – "What do you mean Shreyas by 'present it to him', Shreyas?"

Shreyas said – "We shall put it in a bag and I shall take it to their house."

Mohinder immediately saw the brilliance of the plan and was excited – "Brilliant, Shreyas! That will teach him a lesson, indeed. But you don't have to do it. I know one Security Guard who I think will gladly do it for us. You show me the basement area where you have seen the dog poop and his house, and I shall arrange the rest."

Shreyas immediately took Mohinder Uncle to show him both the places.

All is Well

The 'treatment' of the errant dog-owner started from the next day. The man got the message after a few days of finding a plastic bag containing his dog's poop outside his apartment door every day. Ashamed at last, he also went to a shop and bought a scoop and packets to dispose of his dog's poop. In a few days, the basement became cleaner and started smelling better.

Within a fortnight, not a single paper or plastic bag or dog's poop could be seen anywhere in the Complex. 'Swachh Bharat' had truly begun in their area.

One day, Mohinder Taneja met *Baba* in the Complex. He gave a very warm smile and said – "Akash, your son is truly remarkable. At such a young age, he has done wonders. I have learnt a great lesson from him myself."

From then on, Mohinder Uncle became a very good friend of Shreyas and the other children.

3. Watch and Catch

Bottle Lost – One More!

Tejas and Shreyas came home one evening a bit later than usual after playing football. *Mamma* was worried and had just been about to go down to look for them herself, when she saw them trooping up the staircase to their eighth-floor apartment. *Baba* had specifically instructed them not to use the elevator by themselves, unless another adult was with them. The elevator nowadays had a habit of suddenly stopping midway and the parents did not want the kids stuck on their own in case it happened unexpectedly. Many people had been stranded in the lift for more than half an hour sometimes.

Mamma was a little annoyed as she had instructed the boys many times that they must be home before dark.

Tejas at seven and a half years was generally more compliant to his elders' instructions, but the five-year old Shreyas sometimes took liberties if he got immersed in the games downstairs.

Mamma met them at the door and asked – "Kids, why are you so late today? Didn't I tell you to come home before it gets dark?"

Tejas was clearly agitated about something, but sensing his mother's anger said – "Sorry *Mamma* for being late. But something happened today and we really couldn't help it."

Mamma asked Tejas – "What happened?" She was sure that Tejas would give her all the factual details, though the younger one, Shreyas, had the mischievous habit of coming up with fantastic and made-up stories sometimes. Not that he meant any harm by it. It was still one of those childish habits he had not yet outgrown.

Tejas said – "Rakesh lost his new water-bottle today at the play area."

Mamma was curious and asked – "How did he lose it?" Tejas had also lost one in the past month and the fancy water bottles the kids wanted these days were not exactly cheap.

Tejas started explaining – "You know that we all take our water bottles when we go to play football. We feel very thirsty while we play."

Mamma got impatient – "Tejas, you don't need to explain this to me. I know this. Tell me what happened with Rakesh's bottle."

Tejas stopped speaking and said – "But *Mamma*, you told me the other day that while describing an incident, I should explain from the very beginning!"

Mamma was lost for words for a while, not knowing whether she should contradict her own instructions, but managed to say – "Okay. Now hurry up and tell me how it got lost?"

Tejas picked up the thread of the evening's incident– "I am coming to the point, *Mamma*. After we had finished playing just when it was getting dark, we came back to our building and were about to start up the staircase when Rakesh announced that his water bottle was not with him. He realized that he had left it in the play area. Since it was already dark, we suggested that we could try to pick it up the next morning. But Rajesh (Rakesh's elder brother) said we should go back and get the bottle. I also decided to go with them. But when we went to that place, the bottle was not there. We searched the whole area but could not find the bottle."

Mamma turned to Shreyas and asked – "And where were you Shreyas? Were you also playing football?"

Shreyas said – "No Mamma, I was not playing football. I was in the play area near the gate. But on my way, I stopped at the place where Dada was playing."

Mamma asked again – "But why did you also get late?"

Shreyas said with a mischievous smile – "I was giving courage to them when they were searching."

Mamma could not suppress an amused smile. The little one was turning out to be quite a character!

She now commanded the boys with finality – "Ok, now freshen up and sit down. You need to finish your homework before dinner."

Before going into the washroom, Tejas said – "You know *Mamma*, a few days back Vinod also lost his bottle in the same play area. Anuj also lost his, the other day. I had lost one last month. So many losses - who is taking them, *Mamma*?"

Mamma said – "I don't know, Tejas. May just be a coincidence. Tomorrow you boys go to the Estate Office and ask them if they've found anything."

No Help from Caretakers – The Kids

Take Initiative

As suggested by *Mamma*, the boys went to the Estate Office the next day before starting their game. The Office was located very close to the play area where they all played football. They were led by Rajesh who was the oldest among the boys. The Estate Officer's name was Manjunath. He was generally a good and efficient person who tried to maintain the Complex as best as possible with his limited staff and resources.

Entering the room where Manjunath was sitting, Rajesh said – "Uncle, my brother's water bottle was kept near our play area yesterday. We could not find it later in the evening."

Manjunath said – "I don't know anything about your water bottle, children. If my people find anything, they would bring it to my office and keep it here."

Tejas asked – "Who would bring it, Uncle?"

Manjunath pointed to his Office Attendant – "Gopi there makes a round every evening and picks up anything lying around unattended and deposits them here." He addressed the man now – "Gopi, did you find a water bottle yesterday?"

Gopi, the middle-aged attendant, said strongly – "No, Sir. Anything I find, I always bring to this office, Sir."

Vinod and Anuj also said – "We have also lost our water bottles, Uncle. Tejas also lost his bottle recently."

Manjunath wanted to help the children, but clearly could not do anything. He felt it would be best to close the conversation and said– "You have heard us, children. We did not find any water bottles and in case we find them, they would be kept in this office. You may collect them from here afterwards. Now, please go and play – we have a lot of work to do."

The boys came back without getting a satisfactory answer and started playing. Shreyas also played football with them that day.

That evening, before going home after the game, Rajesh asked Tejas – "What do you think, Tejas? Who is stealing our water bottles?"

Tejas said somewhat gravely – "I don't know, but we have to catch the thief somehow. It is not fair to steal kids' water bottles."

That night, when they piled into bed at bed time, Tejas and Shreyas started talking in low voices.

Shreyas asked – "*Dada*, any guesses as to who is stealing the bottles?"

Tejas said – "I don't know who is stealing, but I surely know who is not stealing."

Shreyas was surprised by this strange answer – "What do you mean, *Dada*?"

Tejas explained to Shreyas – "See Shreyas, nobody staying in the houses in this Complex will steal a water bottle. Who goes to the play area after it is dark? Not the kids or the parents. They are all back home. That leaves only the maid servants and the Estate Office people."

Shreyas suddenly got excited – "Then I can guess who is stealing! *Dada*, it can't be the maid servants. They also go home before dark and those who are staying here take the children under their care back to their homes before dark. So they are not in the play area after we leave."

Tejas saw Shreyas's logic and agreed– "So, who is it then?"

Shreyas said with confidence – "I think it is that Gopi."

Tejas said – "I also guessed as much. But guessing is not enough. We have to catch him in the act. Otherwise Manjunath Uncle will never believe us."

Shreyas said– "That's right. Let us make a plan."

Tejas sat up in bed – "I have an idea. Tomorrow we shall deliberately leave one nice-looking bottle behind in the play area and leave. But we shall not go home. We shall hide close by and keep watch. As soon as the thief tries to take it, we shall catch him."

Shreyas said – "Nice plan, *Dada*, but we are small children. Even if we catch him stealing, he is much bigger than us. How can we catch him?"

Tejas saw the point – "Yes, that's right. We need an elder with us to catch Gopi. But who will come with us kids?"

Shreyas thought for a few moments and the solution was very obvious in his mind– "I know whom to ask! Mohinder Uncle is a very good friend. He will surely help us if I request him."

Tejas said – "It is a good idea. Why don't you ask him tomorrow?"

Shreyas said – "Okay, *Dada*. No problem."

The boys fell asleep soon after – feeling satisfied that they had a good plan to work on the next day.

Friend Joins the Plot

Next day when the eight boys came down to play at five O'clock, they first discussed the plan that Tejas and Shreyas had hatched the previous night. They all agreed it was a good plan and should be tried the same day. Rajesh offered his water bottle as bait for the thief. It was a good-looking bottle in red, which would surely entice the thief. Shreyas was told to go and talk to Mohinder Uncle to be a part of their plan. Shreyas knew where to find him and went there immediately to talk to him.

Mohinder Taneja was a tall, lean and still handsome Punjabi gentleman about 65 years of age, staying with his son Satinder in the Apartment Complex. He had become very friendly with Shreyas and over the last few months had grown quite fond of 'The Boy Wonder', the nickname he had coined for his young protégé. Shreyas found him talking to a Security Guard near the exit gate and straightaway engaged him – "Uncle, we need your help."

Mohinder loved to have fun with his favourite kid-friend, so he narrowed his eyes to a slit and asked - "And who are these 'we'?"

Shreyas was in a hurry to make him agree – "It's me, Tejas and our football friends. Please Uncle, help us!"

Mohinder was not yet through with his fun though "But only on one condition. Those boys will have to play a football match with you and me on one side and the rest on the other – agreed?"

Shreyas did not see much beyond the question and he was in a hurry to make a deal – "Ok, Uncle! Now will you please help us?"

Mohinder's tall frame crouched in front of his little friend. He playfully ruffled Shreyas's hair, and said in a conspiratorial tone – "I smell an exciting adventure! Shreyas, let us go to that bench over there and talk in secret so that nobody else can overhear us."

Shreyas nodded happily- Mohinder Uncle had agreed to be part of their important plan.

The two of them sat side by side on the bench and Mohinder said – "Now, tell me what is going on and why do you need my help?"

Shreyas then explained about the theft and their plan to catch the thief in the act. Then he explained what help the boys required from Mohinder Uncle.

Mohinder was thoroughly impressed by the boys' resourcefulness and ability to think of a plan like that at their age. He asked with surprise in his voice -"Tell me, who thought up this plan?'

Shreyas smiled brightly "*Dada* and I thought of this plan last night and all the other boys liked it." He was happy that Mohinder Uncle also seemed to like it.

Mohinder patted Shreyas on his back enthusiastically and said "Done! I shall be there with you promptly at six O'clock when it starts getting dark. Now go and keep your parents informed, otherwise they will worry about your delay in returning home this evening."

His part accomplished well, Shreyas came back happily to the play area and informed the other boys.

Laying the Trap and the Capture

At six that evening when it was starting to get dark, the boys stopped the game and left the play area. Rajesh did not forget to leave his red water bottle behind, at a place where it could clearly be seen. They pretended to have left the place, but sneaked back after going around the block. They all hid behind a car parked close by from where they had a clear view of the red water bottle. Mohinder Uncle had joined them there from the other side of the lobby

He had a clear message for the boys – "When you see anybody taking the bottle, you boys are not to utter a sound. Is it clear to all of you?"

There were nods and 'yes'-es from the boys.

Mohinder went on – "If he takes the bottle away, I shall leisurely come out and start walking in his direction as if I'm taking an evening walk and have no interest in what he is doing. He will not suspect anything from me. And after that, I will do whatever is necessary. Only when I blow this whistle, should you boys come out of your hiding place, and not before that. Is that understood?" Saying this, he took out a whistle from his pocket and showed it to them.

The boys again nodded in agreement.

Soon it was very dark, but the boys could still see the water bottle in the diffused light from the street lamps a short distance away. Their wait had started. The boys had all informed their parents about the possible delay in returning home that evening.

After about half an hour, a figure whose face could not be seen very clearly came silently towards the play area. The figure looked around and spotted the red water bottle sitting on a stone platform. The boys' eyes were now used to the darkness to some extent and they could clearly see the person pick up the water bottle and start walking towards the Estate Office. As soon as he did that, Mohinder Uncle made a sharp hand movement to the boys to remain quiet and not to move.

He came out of his hiding place and started walking towards the Estate Office casually. Against the light of the Office, Mohinder could now clearly see the man and identified him as the Estate Office Attendant Gopi. But as anticipated, Gopi did not go to the Office to keep the bottle among the lost and found, but instead walked towards the store room which was behind the Estate Office. This was where the Office staff kept their belongings, when they came in to work. Gopi had not yet spotted Mohinder Uncle approaching the building.

When Gopi came out of the store room without the bottle in his hand, Mohinder was waiting near the entrance of the Estate Office. He casually asked Gopi – "Gopi, my grandson left behind a red water bottle near the play area today. Have you seen it, by any chance?"

Gopi instantly said "No, Sir. I did not see any water bottle."

Mohinder asked again "Are you sure?"

"Yes Sir. If I find anything lying around in the evening, I always bring it and keep it in Manjunath Sir's Office."

That was when Mohinder blew his whistle – a signal for the boys to come out and join him.

As the boys all piled out of their hiding place, Mohinder caught hold of Gopi and they all entered the Office of the Estate Manager, Manjunath.

Mohinder now addressed the surprised Manager – "Mr. Manjunath, we have caught the thief red-handed today. He is none other than your Office Attendant Gopi." Then he described the entire drama to the startled Manager.

A thorough search of the store room revealed many missing articles, carefully kept packed and hidden in a box in the cupboard, and ready to be taken away at a convenient time by Gopi. Among these were Rakesh, Vinod, Anuj and Tejas' water bottles.

It was left to the Manager to decide on the punishment to Gopi for his misdeeds.

When they all came out of the Office, Mohinder Uncle took them a little distance away. Seeing their excited and triumphant faces, he asked them a question – "Now that we have caught the thief, can any of you tell me why I did not catch Gopi when he took the bottle and started walking away?"

As the boys started looking at each other, Shreyas raised his hand. Mohinder was expecting this, and said – "Yes Shreyas."

Shreyas said – "You wanted to see where he keeps the bottle. He could have been taking it to the Estate Office like he is supposed to."

Mohinder clapped and said – "Exactly! Very clever of you, Shreyas! Now I have another question." Everybody was eager to know what would come next from him. Mohinder asked –

"Even after I found that he did not keep the bottle in the Office, but took it to the back-room, why I did not blow the whistle to catch him then?"

This time Tejas raised his hand.

"Yes, Tejas?" – asked Mohinder Uncle.

Tejas said – "You had to be sure that it was a 'theft'."

Mohinder Uncle again clapped and smiled– "Right again! I had to give him the benefit of the doubt. If I had accused him then, he could have always said that he had kept it in the store room by mistake, and that he had no intention of stealing. But when I asked him about the red water bottle and he said that he had not seen it, I was absolutely sure that he was stealing it. That's when I blew the whistle."

The boys realized how clever, but fair, Mohinder Uncle had been.

Before leaving, Mohinder Uncle said – "Well done, boys! All credit to you for coming out with a good plan. From now, your water bottles should be safe."

The boys all gathered around and congratulated Tejas and Shreyas for thinking up a good plan, and Shreyas in particular, for roping in Mohinder Uncle to make it such a grand success.

That evening, Tejas and Shreyas did a 'High Five' again. *Baba*, *Mamma* and *Ajji* looked on with surprise on their faces.

4. Problem at School

A Worrying Problem

It was about an hour after lunch at the VIRGO School. In Class II (second grade), a few students suddenly discovered one of their classmates Nitin holding his abdomen and crying in pain. Tears were streaming down his face.

Their previous class had just ended, and the teacher for the next period had not yet come in. A few boys gathered around Nitin trying to give him water to see if it would help. They all felt sorry for him, but did not know what action to take. It was obvious that Nitin was having stomach cramps.

In a few minutes, the new teacher Mansi Ma'am came to the class and found about half a dozen boys crowding around the huddled Nitin. She asked – "What happened boys? Why is Nitin crying?"

As the boys cleared the way for her to investigate, she realized that Nitin was in terrible pain. She knew what to do immediately. She personally took the boy to the Medical Room next to the Principal's Office, where the school Nurse could take a look at him. She made him lie down and informed his parents immediately to come and take him home, or get him medical attention.

As per the rules set by the School, only external injuries were treated by the School Nurse with the first-aid kit in the Medical Room. For all other problems, the School informed the parents and did not give any medicines, since they were not equipped to diagnose what was wrong with the child.

In all such cases, the best course was to inform the parents, who could then choose how they wanted to handle it. In case the parents could not be contacted immediately, then one of the Doctors on the School's contact list would be asked to come down and check on the child. Mansi Ma'am had done exactly as the school procedure dictated.

Fortunately, in Nitin's case, his mother was a homemaker and could drive down immediately. She was at school within fifteen minutes and took her son away for immediate medical attention. All this while, the Teacher remained with Nitin keeping an eye on his condition.

In the meantime, the class buzzed with excitement at what had happened, and all the boys in the class were talking among themselves in the teacher's absence.

Apurv, who was sitting next to Tejas, said – "Tejas, my stomach is also not feeling so great, though it is not as bad as Nitin's. I don't know what's wrong - I was alright in the morning."

Tejas was already mulling over this problem in his head and said – "Apurv, this is happening quite regularly now. Yesterday, it was Justin and he has not come today. Before that it was Puneet and today it has happened to Nitin. Something is wrong!"

Apurv said – "To tell you frankly, I feel OK during the weekends but always feel a little uneasy after our lunch at school."

Tejas was in serious thought – "Do you think it could be the lunch we eat at the school canteen?"

Apurv said – "It could be, but how do we find out?"

Tejas said – "I don't know yet, but we have to find a way. This can't go on."

Apurv said – "Can't we simply inform the teachers? They can find out."

Tejas's reply was quick – "They are so busy with teaching and conducting exams! They're constantly rushing from one class to another. At the end of the day, they're in a hurry to get back to their homes. They don't really have the time to do this extra investigation. If anything, we will have to find the evidence and then inform the teachers so that they can take action."

As they saw Mansi Ma'am walking back towards the class, Apurv said to Tejas – "Let's think about how we can quickly find out what's happening and do something about it. Let us discuss this again tomorrow. I think a whole bunch of our classmates may be interested."

Looking for Solutions

After getting home that evening, Tejas started thinking about the problem. He realized that he and Shreyas never had any stomach trouble from the food cooked at home by their cook Ramakant. Just that moment, Ramakant came into their apartment to cook their dinner.

Without a specific goal in mind, Tejas also entered the kitchen to observe Ramakant while he cooked. He recalled that when he was much younger, he loved to play with the kitchen utensils and used to fight with their previous cook for the pressure cooker. Tejas would only be pacified when the cook washed the pressure cooker after cooking and gave it back to him to play with. As he grew up, slowly Tejas had gotten over his fascination for pressure cookers. Now these memories never failed to bring a smile to his face.

Today, with the school incident very much on his mind, Tejas started thinking–'If we are fine with the food cooked by Ramakant, it must be properly done as per instructions given by *Mamma* and *Ajji*. Let me make note of what he is doing to make our food safe.' He noted a few observations.

1. Ramakant had washed his hands with soap as soon as he came in, before touching anything in the kitchen.

2. Before starting the cooking, Ramakant had thoroughly washed with water the utensils he was going to use.

3. Ramakant checked the raw rice and dal for any insects and washed both multiple times with water before cooking it.

4. All the vegetables were thoroughly washed before being cut and after they were cut, Ramakant did not wash them again.

5. He had covered the pots while cooking was in progress.

6. Ramakant used a fresh hand towel to wipe his hands before taking any spice containers from the cupboard.

7. He never touched food items with his hands after they were prepared.

8. He always wore clean clothes and used an apron while cooking.

9. He kept every vessel containing cooked food properly covered before leaving.

10. He left the apron he was using to be washed, so that he could use a fresh one every day.

As he mentally made notes on his observations, certain ideas started forming in Tejas's mind. He went downstairs to play football with his friends with a satisfied feeling.

Kids Get Together

When Tejas got into the school bus the next morning, he was excited and impatient to discuss his ideas with his classmates. On reaching his school, he immediately found Apurv, Salim and Madhava (as anticipated, Nitin was absent that day). There were still a few minutes before the school start bell went off. The four went into a huddle, and Tejas started explaining – "I think the problem is the food in our canteen. All our friends have fallen sick only after lunch eaten in the canteen." The others nodded in agreement.

Tejas went on – "We have to find out how our food is being prepared in the canteen kitchen. Yesterday in the evening, I watched our cook preparing the food in our house. None of us fall sick after eating the food prepared by him, because he follows some good instructions given by my mother and grandmother. The cooks in our canteen may not be following proper hygiene, and that could be the reason why many of our friends are falling sick."

Salim asked – "But how do we find out?"

Tejas said – "We have to go into the kitchen and see for ourselves when they are preparing the food."

All the other three said – "But who will allow us to enter a hot kitchen with multiple fires and hot oil and while the food is being cooked? We are still kids."

Tejas had already anticipated this problem and had a plan in mind. He said – "I have a plan, but it will require our Class Teacher's co-operation. Let me explain it to you."

After Tejas explained his plan, the four classmates discussed for a while. Questions were asked and answers came out through discussions. At the end, they felt that the plan could work with a little bit of luck.

They quickly filed into the classroom as the school bell had sounded already.

When their social sciences teacher came to teach their class, Tejas got up and asked for permission to speak. As the surprised teacher, Nandini Ma'am nodded, Tejas said – "Ma'am, we eat our lunch in the canteen everyday but have never seen how our food is prepared. If we see that, we shall know many things about our food that you have been trying to teach us through textbooks."

Nandini Ma'am was surprised – "But you are young children. Who will allow you to go into the kitchen with its fire, hot oil and so many other dangerous items?"

Tejas said – "Ma'am, but we shall not go near the fire or hot oil, but observe from a safe distance."

Madhava took the opportunity and also stood up to speak – "Ma'am, if we visit the kitchen, the cooks will also be happy to see that we take an interest in their work."

Nandini Ma'am said – "How can you go and crowd the kitchen? It is a congested place with many things lying around. This will cause trouble for the cooks and they need to finish their work on time or else none of us get our food."

Now Apurv got up – "Ma'am, we shall not go all together. Each day only one of us will go and observe how they work."

But Nandini was still reluctant – "But whosoever goes, that student will miss the lesson for that day."

Tejas had an answer for that as well– "Ma'am, we shall only watch for fifteen minutes. Afterwards, that student can catch up on the lesson from his/her friends."

Nandini was surprised to see the well thought out arguments and plan of action from the young students. But knowing the risks from such a plan, she was still in two minds. On one hand, allowing small children to enter the kitchen had its risks but on the other hand it would give the students a good idea about food preparation and hygiene. And this was practical learning – so much better than just reading about it. Moreover, the kitchen staff would be happy to see that the children they worked so hard for were interested in knowing about their hard work. After weighing the merits and demerits of this plan, she said – "It is certainly a new idea and it has both good and bad aspects. I am not sure whether I can give you an answer on your request right now. I will have to talk to the Principal and seek her opinion. Now no more talking, let's start our lessons for the day."

The children exchanged glances with each other – at least they had won the first round, their request had not been rejected outright!

The Helpful Facilitator

After the classes were over and the school children had left, Nandini met the Principal. While Nandini appreciated the interest among the children to learn about things beyond the classroom, she was still a little doubtful about the implications.

After narrating what the children of Class II wanted to do, Nandini asked the Principal – "It is a good idea and great for these young children to know about other aspects of life, but I don't know whether it would be safe or proper to let them enter the kitchen area with all its dangers."

The Principal was a very progressive and broad-minded lady, who, during her long career, had seen how all-round exposure could help in children become better and smarter adults.

She smiled and said – "Nandini, I like children who are eager to know practical matters and I would be the first one to encourage them. So, I am in agreement with what you said. Now, before we talk about the issue of them entering the kitchen area, I have a question. The child who goes to the kitchen will miss part of the lesson for the day. Will this not affect their grade?"

Nandini was happy that the Principal supported her. She said – "Not really, Madam. The absence will only be for fifteen minutes for one student in a day. If we let them do what interests them, I think they will also feel responsible and try and catch up on whatever they are missing. In fact, I asked them the same question and they told me they would work with their friends and classmates and catch up on what they missed. I think it shows how much they want to do this."

The Principal said – "In that case, let's go ahead with it. Now let's tackle the problem of these children entering the dangerous kitchen area. First, we have to set a '*Laxman Rekha*' beyond which the children cannot enter. That can be fixed by the Canteen Manager based on what he thinks is safe. Secondly, we have to anyway have his agreement to allow the children in the kitchen area. Do you get my point, Nandini?"

Nandini nodded – "Yes, Madam. How do we do that?"

The Principal said – "We can settle the matter right now. Let me call him." She instructed her Secretary to summon the Canteen Manager to her Office immediately.

The Canteen Manager came within a few minutes and was told about the decision taken to let the second-grade children visit the kitchen area. The Principal posed a question to him – "If we go ahead with this, can you assure me that it will not affect your work in any way? Secondly, you have to also draw the line up to which the children can enter, keeping their safety uppermost in your mind."

The Canteen Manager, Narasimhaji was basically a nice person for whom any wish expressed or any decision handed down to him by the Principal was a command and was not to be questioned. He respected her tremendously for her untiring work with the children. He nodded and said – "Madam, only one child coming there in a day will not affect our work in any way. They can enter all areas except where proper cooking is done involving hot oil and fire. They can watch the cooking area from a little distance from where they can see everything but will be safe."

The Principal had got her answers! The Canteen Manager was told to expect one child each day starting the next day. He was then excused and instructed to go back to his work.

The Principal turned to Nandini – "Nandini, I am beginning to like this experiment. This gives me ideas for a few more programs I'd like to start if this is successful. You can start arranging these visits from tomorrow."

The Plan and the Teamwork

The moment the school bus reached school the next morning, Tejas and his friends huddled together. He had worked out a plan during the previous night. He now shared his plan with his classmates – "In case we are allowed to go to the kitchen, we have to observe how the work is being done there. Our observations should be on hygiene only and not on what or how they are cooking. If we feel something is being done in an unhealthy way, we should not say anything, but note it down. I shall gather each of your observations after each day's visit. At the end of twenty days when all the students are done, we shall discuss all our observations and then tell Nandini Ma'am. Is it OK?"

Everybody nodded. Tejas then said – "If we get the permission, let Apurv go today. I shall go tomorrow and after that we can decide who goes when."

The boys were thrilled at the elaborate plan they had put together.

When Nandini Ma'am came to the class that day, she gave the students the news that the Principal had agreed to the visits and it was to start from that same day. The boys expressed their joy by a loud 'Thank You Ma'am' in chorus.

Nandini Ma'am then asked – "Who is volunteering today?"

Apurv raised his hand immediately as agreed earlier in the morning.

Nandini was amazed. Clearly, the children had already planned their visits in anticipation! She said- "I shall take you personally to the Canteen Manager Narasimhaji. He will tell you where you can go and where you cannot. You have to obey him and follow all his instructions – do you understand?"

Apurv nodded in agreement.

Nandini Ma'am continued –And it will be no more than fifteen minutes. When Narasimhaji asks you to return, you come back here immediately, okay?"

Apurv again nodded.

Nandini Ma'am then addressed the class – "After I take Apurv there, I shall be back in five minutes. You children keep quiet in the class and behave. If I find you kids are creating a noise and not behaving yourselves, no visits from tomorrow. Do I make myself clear?"

There was a chorus of 'Yes Ma'am' from the class.

When Nandini came back after leaving Apurv with Narasimhaji, she found the classroom absolutely quiet. She was very pleased!

Observe, Note and Act

The boys' visits to the canteen kitchen went on for the next twenty days. They were thrilled to see many new things they had not seen before – how rice was cooked, how *rotis* were prepared, how *vadas* were fried etc. at such a large scale. They had no idea that all the children in the school ate so much food! For the first time, they saw how hard the canteen staff had to work to provide food to them at the correct time. Narasimhaji was most helpful and personally took the children around every day to explain things. The boys were very happy that they could make these visits possible.

But they did not lose track of their main purpose – to look into the hygiene issues while the food was being prepared. Every day the student visiting the kitchens would come back and narrate his observations of the day to Tejas, who would note it down.

After twenty days, the class was ready. Nandini Ma'am declared that the next day they would skip the regular lesson and the class would discuss what the children had learnt from their kitchen visits.

Tejas had a lot of work to do the night before. Since he had taken the responsibility for collecting all the observations made by his classmates, he now had to put them together in an organized way for presentation to Nandini Ma'am. Not having done this kind of task before, he took some advice from *Baba* and completed his task before going to sleep.

Wonderful Teamwork and Result

As expected, in the classroom the next day Nandini Ma'am addressed the class – "Children, now that we are done with your visits to the canteen kitchen, let us discuss what we learnt there. First of all, let me congratulate all of you. You have all been very disciplined and well-behaved - Narasimhaji told me that."

There was 'Thank you Ma'am' chorus from all the children.

Nandini Ma'am went on – "We have two options now. Either you tell me about your observations one by one, or one of you can collect all your observations and tell me. How do you want to do it?"

The class instantaneously shouted Tejas's name – 'Tejas, Tejas, Tejas' -, who got up and said – "Ma'am, I have already collected and put together all our observations. With your kind permission, I can talk about them."

Nandini Ma'am was pleasantly surprised to see such good teamwork by her class. She nodded to Tejas to go ahead.

Tejas started speaking – "Nandini Ma'am, thank you very much for letting us do this. We learnt many new things in the kitchen. The uncles, who work there, work very hard to give us food on time. From now on whenever we eat food in the canteen, we shall remember those uncles and thank them in our minds. Narasimha Uncle is a very nice person. He was very helpful and explained a lot of things to us when we asked questions. But it is very hot inside, due to which the cooks sweat a lot. There should be more fans. The exhaust fans in the cooking area were also not working.

Ma'am, we are not complaining, but we noticed a few things which need improvement. These are:-

1. Vegetables are not being washed properly before cooking.

2. The cooks are not wearing caps. Some hair may fall on the food.

3. They are not always washing their hands before touching the food.

4. Their aprons are dirty and the same ones are being worn for multiple days. Sometimes they wipe their hands on the apron and then touch the food.

5. The cloths for wiping the steel plates are dirty.

6. The prepared food items are left open without covering. Dust may fall on the food before it is served. We also saw flies sitting on the food."

Tejas thus listed all their observations. He thanked Nandini Ma'am again and sat down.

Nandini Ma'am was impressed beyond words. These young children had done what was essentially the job of a Food Inspector. All the points mentioned were very valid and could be corrected without any major expenditure. She now realized why these children had pleaded to visit the canteen kitchen. It was a well-planned move by them! No doubt their observations were going to be slightly embarrassing for the School Management, but correcting them would be good for everybody.

Nandini noted the points mentioned by Tejas on the blackboard and made up her mind to take them up with the Principal, so that they could see how these problems could be corrected. Given these hygiene issues, no wonder incidents of students falling sick after lunch had become so frequent in the last few months. She felt thankful that no major tragedy had taken place.

She smiled and addressed the class again – "Thank you boys for being so observant and pointing out where improvements are needed. I think that this little experiment we all did together has been very successful. I shall take up these points with our Principal and see what can be done."

At the end of the period when the students were alone, they all 'High Five'd each other.

The Positive Management Takes Action

Nandini did as she had promised. She took up the matter with the Principal. The Principal was equally happy – the new experiment had certainly turned out to be fruitful. That gave her further resolve to try other experiments she had thought about earlier. But a question came to mind – "Nandini, does it mean that our Canteen Manager has been a little negligent to let all these things happen?"

Nandini thought about this for a while and gave her honest and fair opinion – "May be so, Madam, but he is a good and sincere person and has had a lot of responsibilities for so many years. He cares about the students and has always done a good job. I'm sure that once we tell him about the areas which need improvement, he will certainly carry them out and take it in the right spirit. On our part, we also need to create a comfortable and better environment for them to work in."

The Principal was reassured. She certainly did not want to punish Narasimhaji who had been with the school for many years and had always worked sincerely without complaining about the discomfort in the work area.

After that, things happened very fast. The Principal took up the issues with the Canteen Manager and gave instructions for improvement immediately. Narasimhaji, being the person he was, did not hold any grudge against the little visitors who had been instrumental in pointing out these issues. He even suggested such visits once in a while to point out the areas needing improvement.

With the approval of the School Management Committee, the Principal got new fans installed in the canteen, got the exhaust fans repaired and to the delight of the Canteen Staff, got them brand new uniforms, caps and aprons in multiple sets so that they could always wear fresh ones every day.

Within a month, the incidences of boys getting sick after lunch came down drastically.

The Appreciation

During the Annual Function at VIRGO School a few months later, the Principal announced a special citation for the students of Class II for solving a hygiene problem in such a direct manner through their leadership and teamwork. She asked the other students to follow this example.

5. Taming a Bully

The Unhappy Mother

Tejas and Shreyas came back from school at four-thirty. Razia Aunty received them at the bus stop and brought them home. This was the daily routine from Monday to Friday for the boys.

Once they were back home, Tejas went to the bathroom to wash his face and hands before their evening snack and Razia walked into the kitchen to prepare *bhel puri* for them. Shreyas sat down on a chair, removed his shoes and kept them at the proper place in the shoe rack. Next, he took out the empty tiffin-box from his school bag and went inside the kitchen to hand it over to Razia for washing. He realized that something was odd – Razia Aunty was sitting on a small stool in the kitchen with a sad face and was occasionally wiping her eyes with her dupatta.

Razia was the domestic help in the Joshi household and had been working there for the last five years. She had seen the boys, Shreyas in particular, from when he was a little baby and had seen him grow up. She was quite fond of both of them. The boys also liked her and she was treated as a member of the household. Razia usually came in at eight in the morning and left for her home only in the evening. She took full care of the boys and routinely gave them snacks and milk after their return from school.

Being sensitive to people's moods, Shreyas had noticed earlier that she was not up to her usual chatter on the way back from the bus stop as well, but thought Razia was perhaps not feeling very well. But it seemed like the problem was something else altogether.

Shreyas changed his school uniform for more comfortable clothes (he preferred soft pajamas more than the slightly rough jeans) and waited for Tejas to finish freshening up. *Ajji* was resting as she had undergone her knee operation a few days back. Rightly, Shreyas did not want to disturb her.

As soon as Tejas came out, Shreyas went up to him and asked – "*Dada*, have you noticed something?"

Tejas was usually more focused on his own world of books and sports and was not as observant as Shreyas. He said – "Yes, I have noticed many things, but what did you have in mind?"

Shreyas quickly said – "I mean something wrong, *Dada*." He did not want to lose his elder brother's attention.

Tejas was inquisitive – "Why? What's wrong?"

Shreyas's voice was full of concern – "It is Razia Aunty – did you not notice?"

Tejas was usually not mindful of such things. He said – "What's wrong with her? I did not notice anything."

Shreyas decided to come out with whatever was there in his mind, and said – "*Dada*, every day when we come back home from the bus stop, on the way she talks to us so much – what happened at school, what was there for lunch at the canteen, and questions like that. Is it not?"

Tejas said casually – "Yes - so?"

Shreyas's voice was again full of concern – "But today she was quiet all along – didn't ask us even a single question. Didn't you notice that?"

Tejas now saw the point – "Yeah, that's right. Now that you mention it, she was completely silent the entire time."

Having finally got his brother to notice what was wrong, Shreyas pushed on – "Not only that *Dada*, now she is sitting quietly in the kitchen and I think she is crying."

Tejas's face turned serious – "Something must be wrong! We must find out."

Shreyas said – "But how? She'll just tell us not to worry about it if we ask her."

Tejas spoke like the elder brother he was – "Let's not rush it! Let's drink our milk and biscuits like good boys and let's not trouble her today, okay?"

The two brothers ate bananas and drank their milk with biscuits. Razia, while serving, was mostly silent except for a couple of words. As the boys were finishing their snacks on the dining table, Razia again went inside the kitchen and sat down on the stool.

After finishing their milk, Tejas looked at Shreyas and motioned with his eyes towards the kitchen. Tejas whispered to his younger brother – "Shreyas, go on. Ask her now." Tejas knew that Shreyas was so sincere that he was better at getting others to open their hearts out.

As the two of them went into the kitchen and stood before Razia. She looked up and Shreyas asked – "Razia Aunty! Is anything wrong?"

Razia quietly wiped her eyes and got up. She tried to smile as she told the boys in an uncertain voice – "Oh, it's nothing really. Don't you children worry about it."

Shreyas held Razia's hand and spoke in as sincere a tone as he could muster – "But Razia Aunty, we want to help you!"

Tejas also went to her and said in a reasoning tone – "Razia Aunty, please tell us. If we cannot help you, we can ask Baba or Mamma for help. Please, aunty!"

Seeing the sincerity and earnest desire to help in the boys, Razia sighed and said – "It's about my son Jamal, he is very unhappy."

The boys knew that Jamal was only a couple of years older than Tejas. He had come to the Joshi household a couple of times with his mother. He seemed to be a very well-behaved bright kid.

The boys were surprised to hear this from Razia. She had never had issues with Jamal. They asked in unison – "Why, Aunty?"

Razia sighed again and said – "He comes home from school every day hungry and crying."

Shreyas asked– "Why, Aunty? You don't give him tiffin?"

Razia said – "Yes, I do. But he says everyday somebody takes the box out of his bag and eats his tiffin. During the snack break, he finds the box empty. The poor boy gets to eat nothing in the school the whole day."

Tejas asked – "Why doesn't he eat at the school canteen like we do?"

With a strained smile, Razia said – "No, it is a poor boys' school. We can pay only small fees, and with that, only the teachers' salaries can be paid. So, they can't afford to give lunch to the children. I send food with Jamal everyday – lunch and a snack."

Shreyas asked with a serious face – "But who steals Jamal's tiffin?"

Razia shook her head – "I asked him that question. He does not know for sure."

Tejas asked – "But does he suspect anybody?"

Razia nodded – "He thinks it could be Pasha, the strong boy and the class bully."

Tejas asked again in his typical way of trying to put a reason to all actions – "Any reason for suspecting Pasha?"

Razia said with some emphasis – "He is the most aggressive boy in the class who has done many bad things. Moreover, the day Pasha is absent in the class, Jamal's tiffin is not stolen.

So I think Jamal is right, it is Pasha stealing his food everyday."

Shreyas's face reflected the pain he felt for Jamal– "Then why doesn't he complain to the teacher?"

Razia's face showed sadness – "Some other boys had complained to the teacher about Pasha when he stole things from them. Not only did the teacher not punish him, but those boys were later beaten up by Pasha outside the school."

Tejas asked – "But why didn't the teacher punish Pasha?"

Razia sighed again – "Pasha's father Akbar is a local *goonda* and has many connections with the leaders in politics and the police. Everybody is very afraid of him."

Tejas asked – "But Aunty, why has Pasha chosen Jamal only for stealing the tiffin?"

Razia said with a faint smile even at telling the kids about the distressful incident – "Maybe he likes the taste of the food I make! But I think there's another reason. Once Pasha had done something bad in the class and when the teacher asked the boys to identify the culprit, all the boys kept quiet out of fear. But Jamal had the courage to speak the truth. As a result, Pasha was given some light punishment. I think that is why he is targeting Jamal with his mischief."

Both Tejas and Shreyas thought for a moment about what could be done. Where the school teacher and others had been afraid to take action, what could the two little boys do?

Tejas said after some time – "We feel sorry for Jamal. But Aunty, don't worry, we will think of something to help."

Razia's face brightened a little bit - seeing the children's concern for her problem. Also, she felt better after sharing her mental anxieties with someone else. It did not matter that it was with only two little children. She now said – "*Beta*, don't trouble yourself about this. The Almighty will somehow take care of this problem."

Kids Keen to Help

Tejas and Shreyas came back to their room after talking to Razia.

Shreyas said – "*Dada*, Razia Aunty takes such good care of us. We should also do something to make her happy."

Tejas nodded – "Yes, that's right. But how do we teach that bully Pasha a lesson?"

Shreyas said – "Can't we tell *Baba* to complain to the Principal?"

Tejas shook his head – "No, that will not work. Jamal may again get beaten up by Pasha and his friends outside the school. Did you not hear about Pasha's father being a *goonda?*"

Shreyas was not very familiar with the term goonda and asked – *"Dada,* what is a *goonda?"*

Tejas was better informed and said – "A *Goonda* is a daredevil person who beats up other people even for small reasons or no reasons sometimes. He also demands money from others. Even policemen are sometimes afraid to touch them."

Shreyas now understood – "Ah, now I understand what Razia Aunty was trying to say. So, let's think of some other way." He started thinking seriously and after a few minutes an idea suddenly occurred to him.

Tejas was getting ready to go down and play football with his friends. Shreyas sought him out and said – *"Dada,* one day we can tell Razia Aunty to mix a lot of chilies in Jamal's food in the tiffin-box. That Pasha will learn a lesson once he eats that tiffin." He started laughing to himself thinking about Pasha's reaction to the chillies.

Tejas shook his head – "No, Shreyas. That will not work either. One bite of the tiffin and he will not touch it again. Jamal also cannot eat that spicy tiffin, and this happening just one day is not a good enough lesson for Pasha."

Shreyas seeing the point, turned serious again – "Then how do we make sure that Pasha never touches Jamal's tiffin again?"

Tejas said – "It should be such a shocking lesson for Pasha that he will never go anywhere near Jamal's tiffin again. That is the only way it will work."

Shreyas asked – "How do we do that?"

Tejas said – "Nothing comes to mind now. Let's go and play football."

Idea Takes Shape

That night, the two brothers were eating their dinner quietly, mulling over the problem in their heads. Since Shreyas was deeply absorbed in his thoughts, he ate all his vegetables, which he did not do very frequently. Mamma also quietly observed that Shreyas did the right thing that evening. There was no such problem with Tejas as he always ate whatever was put on his plate, including a lot of vegetables.

Baba was not able to eat much that night. He had been having nagging stomach cramps all day. He had been having severe constipation for the past three days. He asked *Mamma* – "Aditi, do you remember my father used to take a medicine for such problems and it used to work very well for him? Do we have that in the house now?"

Mamma said – "Yes, I remember and I know where that medicine is kept. Do you want it now?"

Baba nodded and *Mamma* got up to get the medicine from the small cabinet near the kitchen where all the medicines were kept. She came back a few moments later and gave the bottle to *Baba* and said – "Please remember to take only one spoonful. If by mistake you take two spoonfuls, you will have severe loose motions. That's what the Doctor had advised your father, and truly, he did have a severe loose motion problem once when he took two spoonfuls by mistake. So, be careful!"

Baba nodded and said – "Ok, I shall take only one spoonful and make no mistake about it. But tell me, does it smell awful or have a bad taste?"

Ajji was also having her dinner at the table. She answered – "No bad taste or smell at all. I have also taken it a couple of times. You won't even feel like you are taking any medicine."

Baba smiled as he felt relieved. He did not usually like the smell or taste of any medicine and made a lot of fuss if he was forced to take anything as a last resort.

Listening to the conversation between his parents, Shreyas got the spark of an idea. He made a mental note of the look of the bottle and while he could not read or pronounce the full name of the medicine, he made note of some of the letters in the name as *Mamma* kept the bottle near *Baba*.

That night in bed, Shreyas told Tejas – "*Dada*, I have an idea about how we can teach a fitting lesson to Pasha."

Tejas was immediately excited – "Is it? Tell me, Shreyas." His voice was a little louder.

Shreyas immediately put his hand on his elder brother's mouth – "Be careful, *Dada*. If *Baba* or *Mamma* comes to know what we are trying to do, that will be the end of my idea."

Tejas was sorry and spoke softly – "Yes, sorry Shreyas. Now tell me about your idea!"

Shreyas then explained his plan to Tejas and said at the end – "How do you find my plan?"

Tejas was a little doubtful – "I agree that it's a good plan to teach that bully a lesson. But will Razia Aunty agree to do it?"

Shreyas replied -"I think she will agree in the interest of Jamal. Right now, she does not know what to do and that is troubling her greatly."

Tejas said – "Ok, let's talk to her tomorrow."

Feeling happy for the first time in the whole evening, the two brothers went to sleep.

A Daring Plan

The situation was very much the same the next day also. Tejas and Shreyas found Razia Aunty in a mood similar to the day before. But now they knew the reason and were ready with a plan of action.

Shreyas asked Razia – "Aunty, did Pasha take Jamal's tiffin again yesterday?"

Razia's sad face said everything. She just nodded.

Shreyas asked again – "What are you going to do now, Aunty?"

Razia shook her head – "I don't know. I can't bear him being bullied in school and coming home hungry everyday. It would be better to shift him to another school – but it will involve a lot of expenditure for us. The other schools are very far away from our house also."

Tejas said confidently – "Razia Aunty, you don't have to do that. We have thought of an excellent solution to your problem."

Razia was surprised – "You have found a solution? How strange!" She was amused that the two little boys had found a solution to her biggest problem.

She said – "Ok, tell me what you boys have thought of."

Tejas said – "But before that, tell us who is Jamal's true friend in his class?"

Razia thought for a moment and said – "His best friend is Khaled. He also stays very close to our house."

Tejas said – "Excellent! Now Aunty, please tell us which dish you prepare best?"

Razia said – "Vegetable *Upma* - everybody loves it. I also put a lot of dhania leaves which give a nice taste to the *Upma*."

Tejas now looked straight into Razia's eyes and started explaining the plan – "Aunty, tomorrow you make your best vegetable *Upma*, but give two tiffin-boxes to Jamal for school. One is for Jamal, which you ask Khaled to keep with him. In that box, you put a little extra *Upma* so that Khaled also can have some along with Jamal. Keep the second box in Jamal's bag."

Shreyas jumped into the narrative here and said – "Just a minute Aunty, let me bring something to show you. Then we can tell you what to do next."

Both the brothers ran out of the kitchen to the Medicine Cabinet. It was at a height beyond the boys' reach, so they brought a stool to stand on and reach up to the Cabinet. Even with the stool it would have been unreachable for Shreyas, so it had to be fetched by his taller elder brother.

Once Tejas climbed up and could see inside the deep Cabinet, Tejas asked – "Shreyas, tell me which bottle you want me to take out?"

Shreyas said – "It is a big blue-coloured bottle with a white cap."

Tejas had a look inside and asked – "Do you remember the name of the medicine?"

Shreyas said – "No *Dada*, I could not read the name of the medicine, but it starts with the letter 'O'."

Tejas searched inside and took out a bottle matching the description given by Shreyas. He showed it to his younger brother – "Is this the bottle?"

Shreyas immediately recognized the bottle as the one *Mamma* had given to *Baba* the previous night – "Yes that is the one! Please bring it down."

Tejas got off the stool with the bottle in his hand. Now he asked Shreyas – "Do you remember how much of this is to be given?"

Shreyas remembered the conversation of the previous night – "*Mamma* told *Baba* to take one spoonful only, but said two spoonfuls taken by mistake would cause severe loose motion. So, what do you think?"

Tejas thought for a moment – his face showed a lot of determination – "Shreyas, we want to teach Pasha the lesson of his life, isn't it?"

Shreyas's face also was serious – "Yes, bullying is a very bad thing and he should learn not to do such mischief again."

Tejas's mind was made up – "We should use two spoonfuls then. That would give him such a shock that he won't go anywhere near Jamal's tiffin-box again."

The two brothers walked into the kitchen with the bottle in Tejas's hand. Shreyas immediately took charge – "Razia Aunty, Jamal will eat his tiffin from the box kept in Khaled's bag – tell him not to make any mistake about it, okay?"

Razia nodded – "Ok, I shall tell him that."

Shreyas continued – "But in the box kept in Jamal's bag, you mix this medicine in the *Upma.*"

Razia was startled – "What is this medicine? What will it do?"

Shreyas said – "Nothing very bad. I have seen *Baba* taking it sometimes when he has problems with his stomach."

Razia was still in doubt – "But what will happen to Pasha? I don't want him to be in any serious trouble."

Shreyas said – "Don't worry, Aunty. It will teach Pasha a good lesson. Don't you want that?"

Razia nodded – "Yes, but still you have not told me what will happen to Pasha."

Now Tejas chipped in – "Razia Aunty, don't worry so much. It will only cause severe loose motion - nothing more."

Razia was in two minds – "Are you sure it will cause no serious harm? He may be a bad boy, but as a mother, I don't want to hurt any child."

Tejas smiled and said – "Please don't worry so much, Razia Aunty. We also want him to learn a serious lesson only, nothing more. He will miss school for the next three to four days but after that he will not touch Jamal's tiffin again."

The last part of Tejas's sentence made an appeal to Razia's mind. She visualized Jamal's pain and unhappiness day after day in having to stay in school hungry. She was more or less convinced now that something had to be done soon. She looked at the medicine bottle and asked – "How much medicine do I have to add to the *Upma*?"

Shreyas said – "Just two spoonfuls – no more, but only to the *Upma* in the tiffin-box in Jamal's bag."

So, the stage was set and the grand plan was put into action the next day.

Putting a Plan into Action

The next day went as planned in Razia's household. She prepared her best-ever *Upma* with a lot of coriander leaves and *ghee*. The aroma of the *Upma* totally covered up the slightest possible smell of the medicine, which she mixed in the tiffin-box to be carried in Jamal's school bag. She repeatedly told her son to eat his tiffin only from the box kept in Khaled's bag. She also packed some *Upma* separately in a box for Khaled – who was called from the neighbourhood to safely keep the two boxes meant for him and Jamal in his bag.

To make Pasha greedier that day to eat his tiffin, as instructed by his mother, Jamal opened the tiffin box kept in his bag before the class started. The aroma of his mother's *Upma* spread through the classroom and Pasha immediately turned his head in Jamal's direction. Seeing Pasha's reaction, Jamal again closed the tiffin-box and kept it in his school bag, with a faint smile on his face.

As per the plan, Jamal afterwards left his bag unattended for the entire break and went off to play. As expected, he came back to find that the *Upma* in his tiffin-box had been polished off by Pasha, who now sat in his seat with a very satisfied expression on his face. Little did he know what trouble awaited him for the next few days!

The next day Tejas and Shreyas found Razia Aunty more cheerful. Now that she was also a part of the conspiracy, she told the boys everything that had happened in the school the previous day. Everything happened as planned. Now wait for the result – she said.

The Tormentor Pays

Now it would be interesting to visit Pasha's household to find out what was happening there.

The morning after Pasha ate that 'Delicious Special *Upma*' from Jamal's tiffin-box, he was in trouble. His stomach started churning and grumbling early in the morning. Three or four visits to the toilet also did not relive the growling and discomfort in his stomach. The pain in his abdomen was becoming more and more intense.

When Pasha's mother Farida came into his room to find out why he was not up yet to get ready for school, she found her son in a total mess – he had his arms wrapped around his stomach and was squirming.

Farida was a short-tempered woman who did not tolerate much nonsense from anybody (otherwise how could she get on in life - being a *'goonda's* wife?). She yelled – "You lazy boy! Get up and get ready fast!" She started a threatening move with the stick she usually carried in her hand around the house.

With great difficulty, Pasha got up, but finding the pain to be too much, held his stomach and started crying – "My stomach! My stomach! I'm in terrible pain!" Tears were streaming down his face.

Farida understood that her son was suffering from a severe stomach upset. She said – "But I gave you nice food from home yesterday! Did you eat anything outside? Tell me the truth!"

The difficult boy was already softened by his stomach pain. He started crying – "Sorry *Ammi*. I shall tell you the truth. I ate Jamal's tiffin yesterday."

Farida lowered her stick and asked suspiciously – "Did Jamal give you the tiffin?"

Pasha now had to tell the truth – "No, I stole it from his bag."

Farida found this difficult to believe – "Was it the first time or do you do it regularly?" Pasha kept silent. He was afraid to come out with the full truth.

The short-tempered mother lifted her stick again – threatening to strike.

He mumbled through his tears – "Many times, *Ammi*! I won't do it again, I promise!"

Farida then yelled at him – "You can suffer with this stomach pain! Who asked you to steal food from other boys? This is the right punishment! No food for you today!" She stomped out of the room angrily and locked it from outside, leaving the boy still squirming in pain.

Pasha remained bedridden for the next three days and came back to school only after one week.

He never went anywhere near Jamal's tiffin again.

The Relieved Mother

After a few days, Razia Aunty was back to her smiling self. She told Tejas and Shreyas quietly that now there were no more problems with Jamal's tiffin being stolen. As a token of her gratitude, one day she brought a tiffin-box filled with her 'Delicious Special *Upma*' which the boys were immensely fond of.

That night, Tejas and Shreyas celebrated their good act by doing another 'High Five'.

6. Don't Pluck the flowers

Uncle States a problem

Tejas and Shreyas were playing football with their friends as usual in the play area. It was nearing the time when the evening light normally fades and darkness sets in. Daily, the boys would end their game around this time, as their parents had strictly instructed them not to play in the dark.

To catch the attention of Shreyas from the stone bench on which he was sitting, a short distance away, Mohinder Uncle raised his right hand and signaled the boy to come to him. Since the game was over, Shreyas immediately ran towards his favourite 'Uncle'. Seeing his younger brother running, Tejas also followed him. At seven-and-a-half, Tejas was conscious of his responsibilities towards his five-year old younger brother.

In many ways now, Mohinder Uncle was a mentor to Shreyas – telling him about many things in life, outside of the regular school studies. The conversations between the two would have sounded hilarious to anybody overhearing them.

As the Joshi brothers came closer, Mohinder Uncle said – "Tejas and Shreyas, it is getting dark. So, let's talk while I walk you back to your apartment building. That way, you will be home before it gets too dark." The Joshis lived on the eighth floor of the G-Block, which was the farthest building from the play area.

As the three of them started walking back, Mohinder Uncle took out two wafers from his pocket and gave them to the kids and started talking – "We have a problem in this Complex, which has to be solved soon."

Tejas asked – "Uncle, is it a difficult problem, or a small problem?"

By now, Mohinder was familiar with Tejas's mental process of being precise and very specific on issues, so he smiled and continued – "That depends on who looks at the problem. To most residents, it is a small problem, but for the person who told me about it, it is a big problem, which is causing a lot of restless nights for him."

Shreyas pulled at Mohinder Uncle's long fingers – "But why don't you tell us about it, Mohinder Uncle?" He loved to utter the old man's name most of the times he addressed him.

Mohinder stopped walking and bent down with some difficulty (because of his spinal problem) to be level with his young friends and said in a hushed tone – "Somebody is stealing flowers from our garden in this complex."

Tejas immediately asked – "Which garden? What flowers?" He wanted to know specifics since there were many scattered plant-beds around the Complex and each bed grew a certain specific type of flower.

Mohinder again smiled at Tejas's pointed question and extended his right hand to point to a big flower bed about fifty feet away – "That garden area, the 'Arabian Jasmine' flowers from that bed are being stolen every day."

Shreyas asked – "But how do you know, Mohinder Uncle, that the flowers are being stolen?"

By this time they were already at the entrance to the G-block Building. Selva, their neighbour on the eighth floor was waiting for them and holding the elevator open. Noticing that, Mohinder said – "Tomorrow is Saturday and a holiday from school. Come down at ten O'clock near the jasmine flower bed. We'll talk then." He left after depositing the kids with Selva. The boys were told by their parents not to travel in the elevator alone without an adult, as the elevator had been breaking down frequently of late.

The Problem

Back in their apartment, Tejas and Shreyas cleaned up, changed their clothes and sat down to do their homework in their room. *Baba*, *Mamma* and *Ajji* were talking among themselves in the living room.

Shreyas was impatient to get to the mystery Mohinder Uncle had told them about. He asked his elder brother – "*Dada*, why are those jasmine flowers being stolen?"

Tejas was busy working on his Math Olympiad work-book and said – "How do I know? Mohinder Uncle will tell you about it tomorrow."

Shreyas said – "Flowers look so nice on the plants, don't they? Why would anybody pluck them?"

Tejas said – "I agree with you, Shreyas. But don't disturb me now, you will know more about it tomorrow from Mohinder Uncle."

Next morning at ten O'clock *Baba* took Shreyas to the spot near the jasmine flower-bed. Mohinder was already there talking to the gardener who was tending to the plants. *Baba* and Mohinder knew each other well and there was no problem in leaving the kid in the custody of the senior man. *Baba* went back home to leave for his piano class at ten thirty. Before coming to meet Mohinder Uncle, Shreyas had been made to finish his breakfast of *idlis* and *sambar*.

Mohinder guided Shreyas to where the gardener was busy removing the weeds from the flower-bed and said – "Shreyas, meet our gardener Mallappa. He has been working here since the time I have moved in. Say '*Namaste*' to him."

Shreyas dutifully joined his palms together and said – "*Namaste*, Mallappa Uncle."

The elderly gardener displayed a wide smile and also joined his palms together. He felt genuinely pleased to see kids showing respect – it was not that common these days.

Mohinder said to Shreyas – "Mallappa tells me that every day early in the morning, someone takes away most of the jasmine flowers from these plants."

Fortunately, Mallappa knew Hindi quite well and they could talk without any problem. Mohinder did not know how to speak Kannada, and though Shreyas had learnt a few words from his friends in school, his grasp of Kannada was not enough to hold a conversation. Mallappa narrated the story of the jasmine flowers. From his long experience, Mallappa knew from the number of buds he observed on the plants on any given evening, the number of flowers that should bloom the next morning on those plants. But when he came in to work at nine in the morning, he could see less than one-fourth of the number expected. There were no flowers dropped on the bed below as well. This clearly meant that someone was plucking these flowers before nine O'clock in the morning. This had been happening on a regular basis.

An idea flashed through Shreyas's mind, and he asked – "Mohinder Uncle, there are many other flower beds in our Complex. Are those flowers being plucked too?"

Mohinder was pleased to observe that his little friend was already putting his thinking cap on. He repeated the question to Mallappa.

Mallappa replied – "No Sir, only jasmine and hibiscus flowers are being plucked, the others are not touched." He suddenly remembered something else and added – "Sir, a strange thing also happens. For one week, more flowers are stolen and the following week less quantity is plucked. This alternating pattern is going on for the last few months. I don't understand this at all!"

Mohinder thought about this last piece of information very seriously and looked at Shreyas with questioning eyes, but the little boy shook his head – he had no idea what it meant.

After finishing their conversation with Mallappa and gathering all the information they could, Mohinder took Shreyas into the shade of a nearby tree (it was beginning to warm up by now). He said – "Shreyas, what have we learnt from our talk with Mallappa?"

Shreyas thought for a few moments and said – "The flowers are being plucked before nine O'clock in the morning, and only jasmine and hibiscus are being stolen. I did not understand what he said about weeks and more or less flowers being plucked, though. But Mohinder Uncle, could those flowers be taken in the evening by any chance?"

Mohinder Uncle shook his head – "No. I had asked the same question to Mallappa. He said that these flowers bloom early in the morning and it is more likely that somebody could be plucking them at that time."

Shreyas asked – "But Uncle, are people allowed to pluck flowers?"

Mohinder again shook his head – "No. There is a clear notice from the Estate Manager asking residents not to pluck flowers from the garden."

They talked for some more time about who could be committing this mischief. Before leaving the spot, Mohinder said – "Shreyas, as responsible residents we cannot let this continue. We have to find out who is doing it and catch him or her. We also are not sure whether it is more than one person. Let us take a day and try and think of a plan to find this out."

Shortly thereafter, Mohinder left Shreyas at his apartment and went back to his own residence.

The Kids Plan Watch

After entering their apartment, Shreyas observed that *Ajji* was preparing for her customary '*puja*' before the small '*Mandir*' in their house. Shreyas liked to observe the rituals while she did so. Afterwards, it was his regular practice to chant the verses along with his grandmother. The last attraction of this '*puja*' was the '*prasad*' that *Ajji* would hand out to him.

What caught Shreyas's attention was that *Ajji* was arranging some white and red flowers on a small tray kept in front of the '*Mandir*'. Since *Ajji* was busy with the arrangements, Shreyas kept quiet and resolved to ask her some questions later.

As soon as the *puja* was over, Shreyas asked her – "What are those flowers, *Ajji*?"

Ajji replied – "Jasmine and hibiscus."

Shreyas asked – "From where did you get them?"

Ajji said – "Oh, Razia brings them every day when she comes for work in the morning." Razia was their domestic help and nanny.

Shreyas then went to the kitchen where Razia was washing the utensils and asked her – "Razia Aunty, from where do you get the jasmine and hibiscus flowers for *Ajji*?"

Razia said – "There is a woman who sells these flowers in front of the shop just outside the gate. I buy the flowers from her for ten rupees which *Ajji* gives me every day."

Shreyas asked again – "Who else buys the flowers?"

Razia said – "Mostly the maids from this Complex, and mostly from the houses where the old people do their 'puja' every day like your *Ajji*."

Shreyas absorbed all this information. Thinking quickly, he decided that it must be one of the maids from the apartment who was the culprit. But the problem was – how were they to identify the culprit and catch him or her in the act?

Later in the day, Shreyas caught hold of Tejas and told him all that happened since morning. Tejas was good at putting things together through logical thought.

After listening gravely to Shreyas, Tejas said – "I think you are right. None of the house owners will send their maids to pluck those flowers from the garden in the Complex. So, that maid must be cheating – plucking the flowers and pocketing the money."

Shreyas said – "Yes, *Dada* – that must be so. But how do we catch the thief?"

Tejas said – "You have to watch and catch. Remember how we caught that water-bottle thief Gopi? Exactly like that."

Shreyas asked – "But when do we watch?"

Tejas was his usual logical self – "Think calmly, Shreyas! Since the flowers bloom in the early morning, it is most likely that they are plucked at that time. Some uncles and aunties go for their morning walk and exercise in the morning. If the flowers are plucked at that time by the thief, he or she will be seen by those walking on the road. So, the flowers must be plucked even before the uncles and aunties start walking."

Shreyas said thoughtfully – "That means we have to start watching the flowers very early."

Tejas nodded – "Yes, but who will go so early in the morning?"

Shreyas promptly said – "I can! I get up very early."

Tejas was not an early riser. Moreover, on Sundays he had to go for his soccer coaching with *Baba*. He said – "Let's do this, Shreyas. *Mamma* goes for her *Yoga* classes very early in the morning on Sundays. You go with her tomorrow and from there keep a watch on the roadside. The windows in the community center look out on to the flower beds and you can spot anybody approaching that area."

Shreyas liked the idea and said he would do as Tejas suggested.

That night, Shreyas said to *Mamma* after dinner – "*Mamma*, at what time do you have to go for your *Yoga* classes tomorrow morning?"

Mamma was surprised by this question from the younger one. She said – "Five O'clock? Why?"

Shreyas innocently said – "*Mamma*, could I also come with you tomorrow?"

Now *Mamma* was really surprised – "But why, Shreyas? What will you do there for an hour and a half?" She knew waking up so early was not a problem for Shreyas as he was an early riser.

Shreyas said – "I want to see how you do your *Yoga*, *Mamma*. Please *Mamma*, just for a day!"

Mamma thought for a few moments. After all, there was no harm in the little kid seeing the *Yoga* practice. She said – "Ok, but put on a sweater and don't stray from the class."

Shreyas nodded, but worked out his own plan for things to do the next morning.

The Observation

Shreyas was dressed and ready (wearing a sweater as well) by the time *Mamma* finished her preparations to go for her *Yoga* class at five O'clock the next morning. She was pleasantly surprised to see her younger child growing up to be so self-reliant. "Let's go", she said, adding – "but remember that you are not to go anywhere alone." Shreyas nodded his head at this repeated instruction.

The *Yoga* class was held in the function room of the Community Center in their Complex. The class started promptly at five minutes past five O'clock. As *Mamma* got busy, Shreyas came outside and sat on a chair in the passage just outside the Function Room. From his position, he could get a direct view of the jasmine flower-bed. He could spot anybody approaching the flower beds and would be able to see who was plucking the flowers. Though it was not daylight yet, there was enough light from the street lamps for him to see clearly.

Nothing happened for the next half an hour. Shreyas was beginning to have doubts whether he would be successful today. But soon after five-thirty, he suddenly spotted a figure walking up to the flower beds and stopping there. Shreyas was excited and started walking towards the window to get a clearer view of the person.

The figure turned out to be that of a young girl stooping over the flower-bed and busy plucking the flowers to put them in a small plastic bag hurriedly. There was no one else on the path to witness this act of stealing. Shreyas hid himself behind a palm tree nearby to observe her secretly.

It took only two or three minutes for the girl to take as many flowers as she needed and then she turned around to go back. Shreyas could now see her face and was surprised to find that he recognized her. She was none other than Manjula, the resident domestic help at the house of his friend Anurag who stayed in the adjacent block. Shreyas decided to remain silent and followed Manjula to wherever she was going next.

Manjula walked back but did not enter the building. Instead she went down the path to the basement parking area. By this time, Shreyas had slipped out of the Community Center and was following her. Once inside, she kept the plastic bag with flowers hidden behind a big pipe and then went to take the elevator to the apartment she was working in.

Shreyas now understood the game she was playing. The flowers had been stolen and hidden away safely. She would later collect money from the mistress of the house to purchase flowers and carry back the stolen flowers – pocketing the money. A very clever plan – he thought.

As per instructions from Mohinder Uncle (he remembered their earlier adventure of 'Watch and Catch'), Shreyas did not do anything at that time, but decided to wait for his meeting with his senior friend in the evening.

Problem Solved

At five O'clock in the evening, Mohinder Uncle came to his usual stone bench to find both Tejas and Shreyas waiting for him there (having come to know of Shreyas's morning adventure, Tejas was also very excited and wanted to be a part of what would happen next).

Even before Mohinder could sit down, Shreyas said excitedly – "Mohinder Uncle, I found the flower-thief."

Mohinder was totally surprised. Barely twenty-four hours had passed since they were speculating about who could commit such an act, and now this tiny kid had found the culprit! He asked eagerly – "Good work, Shreyas! Who is the thief? Someone I know?"

Now Tejas said – "You may not know her Uncle, but we do. She is Manjula Aunty – who stays and works in Anurag's house in H-Block."

Mohinder put his hand on his lips and said in genuine shock – "Oh my God! I know that girl – I have seen her with Anurag sometimes. I also know Anurag's father Adarsh."

Shreyas asked – "What we should do now, Mohinder Uncle?"

Mohinder smiled and patted Shreyas on his back – "You have really done a great job, Shreyas! Now leave the rest to me."

Tejas as usual was anxious to know precisely what action was to be taken. He asked – "But what are you going to do, Uncle?"

Mohinder said firmly – "I know that Anurag's father Adarsh is a good person who would take care of this problem. I shall go to their house myself and do what is necessary. Let me assure you that the jasmine flowers will not be plucked again."

Tejas's exactness was again clear in his next question – "But what about the hibiscus flowers, Uncle?"

Mohinder had a good laugh and patted Tejas on his back as he said – "Oh, hibiscus also. Now you two go and join your friends in your football game. I can see that they are waiting for you."

The boys felt happy that a problem had been solved and went to join their football mates.

As promised, Mohinder went to Adarsh's house the same evening and told him all about the entire episode. Obviously, Adarsh was shocked and immediately called for their resident domestic help, Manjula and asked her about the flowers. As expected, she denied any wrong-doing at first, but confessed in the end when Mohinder talked about an eye-witness without taking Shreyas's name. She started crying and admitted that she had been plucking the jasmine and hibiscus flowers from the Complex garden in the morning and keeping those hidden in the basement. Later on, when Adarsh's mother would give her ten rupees to get flowers from the seller outside the gate, she would bring the stolen flowers up and pocket the money. She told them she was doing this to earn a little extra since her family back in their village needed more money to survive.

Adarsh was a good man at heart. He realized that poor people sometimes had their own personal motives for doing these wrong things. Instead of punishing her (she was otherwise an excellent domestic help), he increased her salary by two hundred rupees a month, but made her promise that she would never do such a thing again.

Mohinder went back a happy person. He was also a kind and considerate man at heart. He was happy that the problem had been solved, but the guilty had been treated compassionately.

But the Problem Persists

After a few days, Mohinder Uncle again called Shreyas and Tejas to his stone bench near the children's play area. The boys could sense that his face was serious and he was not his smiling self.

As the Joshi brothers came closer, Mohinder Uncle looked into their eyes and said gravely – "Tejas and Shreyas, we thought we had solved the flower problem once and for all, but the flower-thief is at it again."

The boys were shocked. Shreyas asked – "Manjula Aunty is plucking the flowers again?"

Mohinder shook his head – "No, not Manjula. I checked with both her and Adarsh last evening. She swore that she had stopped plucking the flowers now." Then he proceeded to tell what had happened during the last two days.

The day before, Mohinder met Mallappa while the gardener was working on the flower beds. Mohinder confidently declared to the gardener that he should be happy now that the flower theft had stopped. He was shocked when Mallappa informed that though the jasmine flower-plucking had reduced, it had not stopped altogether. Still, a large quantity of flowers was being plucked. But he told Mohinder that plucking of the hibiscus flowers had stopped now and only the jasmine flowers were being stolen.

Mohinder's first reaction was to assume that Manjula was still doing the mischief and he had gone to Adarsh's house to check on that. But after hearing Manjula, he had believed her.

Tejas and Shreyas were shocked – "So, who is doing it now, Uncle?"

Mohinder gravely shook his head – "No idea. So, let's be on alert once again. We may have the toughest case on our hands to solve now."

That night in their bedroom, Tejas said – "That means anybody found with white jasmine flowers would be a suspect. Let us keep a watch on everybody."

More Observation

The next day was Saturday and *Mamma* had her *Yoga* class again. Like last Sunday, Shreyas requested to accompany her. Mamma was not averse to her younger son's coming along like the last time and agreed, but imposed the same conditions.

Like on the earlier occasion, Shreyas was on the lookout for anybody approaching the jasmine flower bed. For quite some time, he did not see anyone nearby, but observed a Security Guard keeping vigil in the nearby area. On and off he could see only that man. It was really nice that the Security folks had also recognized this petty theft and decided to keep a patrol nearby. 'It must be due to Mohinder Uncle's request' – thought Shreyas. He was now satisfied that the theft would stop soon with the culprit caught. Mentally satisfied, he came back to where the *Yoga* class was in progress and watched *Mamma* as she did her *asanas*.

The next day, Shreyas came again with his Mamma and was satisfied to see the same routine – the Security Guard was walking up and down the path near the flower-bed. But this time Shreyas went closer to observe the sincere Security Guard. He thought he recognized him as the guard who mostly manned the exit gate.

As Mohinder Uncle was busy with some programme among the Punjabi community in Bengaluru on Saturday and Sunday, Shreyas did not meet him during the weekend.

On Monday morning, Tejas and Shreyas were waiting for their school bus near the Complex gate. They loved to come a few minutes early and meet their friends who studied in another school and also waited for their school bus at the same spot.

Suddenly, Tejas's eyes caught sight of a young woman coming out of the Complex gate and walking away. He urgently caught hold of Shreyas's arm and exclaimed– "Shreyas, look there!"

Shreyas was surprised – "Look where, *Dada?*"

Tejas said – "Look at that Aunty! She has such a big garland made of jasmine tied to her hair!"

Shreyas said – "Why, *Dada*? Girls put flowers in their hair, is it not?"

Tejas said – "Yes, but have you seen any maid putting flowers? Even if they do, it would be one or two flowers – and not such a big garland."

Shreyas said – "That's right, *Dada*. They don't usually put on such large garlands."

Tejas again looked intently in the direction that the woman was walking away – "Do you know her?"

Shreyas nodded – "Yes, she is Shanthi Aunty who works in my friend, Kimaya's house."

A few moments passed. Suddenly, Shreyas got excited and said – "*Dada*, I just remembered something. Yesterday morning when I was returning home with Mamma after her *Yoga* class, I saw Shanthi Aunty coming in for work. But she did not have any flowers in her hair."

Tejas said – "Maybe she does not put them on every day. But it is a good observation – let's keep our eyes open."

The Complex Problem

On Monday evening, Shreyas met Mohinder Uncle again and told him all about the observations he had made on Saturday and Sunday mornings and what he and Tejas had observed in the morning about Shanthi.

Mohinder's face was serious as he said – "Your observations are really good. Keep it up! I was talking to Mallappa again this morning and he says the plucking of flowers is still going on. So, we have to solve this, Shreyas."

Shreyas was surprised. He thought that they had solved the problem! He said – "But Uncle, the Security Guard was walking up and down the path near the flower-bed. How can anybody steal in his presence?"

Mohinder had some thoughts of his own and he absent-mindedly said – "It is still possible. We have to do a serious analysis of the timings. It all depends on who is or are near that place at the time." He continued thinking, and seeing his friend's serious face, Shreyas also sat quiet, letting Mohinder Uncle think.

After a few moments, Mohinder came out of his mental pre-occupation and asked Shreyas – "Do you know the Security Guard, Shreyas? Or at least will you be able to recognize him if you see him again?"

Shreyas nodded – "Yes, I recognize him. Usually he stands guard near the exit gate, but I don't know his name."

Mohinder suddenly came to a decision. He got up and said – "Come on, Shreyas. Let us go and see if he is still there." They walked a short distance to the exit gate.

Fortunately, the same Guard was on duty and Shreyas pointed him out and identified him to Mohinder Uncle.

Since it was Mohinder's habit to casually talk to all the support staff from time to time, he knew the names of almost all of them. The moment Shreyas identified the Guard, he said – "Oh, that one? He is Santosh." The man was in his mid-twenties, slimly built, dark-complexioned and had a thick moustache.

Shreyas asked – "Why has he not gone home? Do they work here all the time?"

Mohinder was surprised that Shreyas was aware of duty hours. He smiled and said – "No, they work on eight hour shifts and their shifts change every week – usually from Monday evenings. So, Santosh will go home at ten O'clock tonight and come back again at six in the morning tomorrow. He must have been on night shift when you saw him on Saturday and Sunday." Mohinder recounted what he knew about the Security System to Shreyas.

They met again on Tuesday morning. Mohinder had information to share with his young friend.

"I have two things to tell you, Shreyas. One, Mallappa said the flowers were not stolen this morning and two, I came to know that the girl you saw with the flowers in her hair, is in fact

Santosh's sister. They stay very near to this Complex in Mangammapalya." What Mohinder did not say was that he had gathered this information by talking to the other Security guards.

Shreyas listened to Mohinder Uncle. The information was interesting, but he could not readily make out what they meant as far as their case was concerned.

But he also had one item of information to share. He and Tejas had also not seen any flowers in Shanthi's hair that morning.

Mohinder Uncle nodded his head at this piece of information from Shreyas and mentally started piecing everything together.

The situation remained the same throughout the week. Mallappa happily reported every evening that flowers were not being stolen and Shreyas reported that Shanthi's hair remained without flowers.

Shreyas had an additional information to pass on to Mohinder Uncle – "Uncle, on Saturday and Sunday also I went with Mamma to her *Yoga* class. But I did not see any Security guard near the flowers."

Hope but Disappointment Again

On the next Monday morning, both Mohinder and Shreyas were in a cheerful mood. They were both now confident that the flower theft had been stopped for good. They celebrated with 'high fives' and Mohinder bought Shreyas a Cadbury chocolate from the shop. Back home, Shreyas declared to his elder brother that the 'flower case' was now closed.

But things took an unexpected turn on Tuesday evening. Mohinder's face was serious and had a worried look when they met at their usual place – the stone bench.

Mohinder said – "Shreyas, we celebrated too soon! The mischief-maker is back! Mallappa said the flowers were stolen again this morning!"

Shreyas could not believe this! He was quiet for a few moments and suddenly something flashed through his mind and he said excitedly – "and do you know Mohinder Uncle – we saw Shanthi Aunty again this morning with flowers in her hair?"

Mohinder looked intently at his tiny friend and his face broke into a strange smile. He hugged Shreyas and said slowly – "Shreyas, this was the last piece of information, which now fits perfectly into our puzzle. I know now what is happening and what is to be done. I only have to gather solid proof. Don't ask me anything now – by this time tomorrow all will be clear to you. Now go and enjoy your football game. The problem is solved now."

Though Shreyas had some idea of what was about to happen, he wasn't sure whether Mohinder Uncle was thinking along the same lines and so didn't say anything. He went and joined his football mates.

The Vital Clue and the Final Solution

While waiting for their school bus on Wednesday morning, Tejas and Shreyas again saw Shanthi coming out of the Complex gate with flowers in her hair. Shreyas remembered what Mohinder Uncle had told him. 'Is there some connection between the plucked flowers and those on Shanthi Aunty's hair?' – was the thought on Shreyas's mind. He also remembered Mohinder Uncle's confident statement that the problem was solved. 'Then why were the flowers seen again in her hair?' – He thought. This question would perhaps only be answered by Mohinder Uncle in the evening, Shreyas thought.

The moment Shreyas returned home from school and finished his fruits, milk and biscuits, he ran downstairs, eager to meet his senior friend and hear about what was happening in their 'flower theft case'. Tejas also came along because he was very keen to know about the case.

Mohinder Uncle was already seated on the stone bench and had a broad smile on his face. The moment the two Joshi kids reached him, he took out a small plastic box and opened it for them. There was one *'rosogolla'* and one *'gulab jamun'* (Mohinder was aware that Shreyas liked *'rosogolla'* and Tejas was fond of *'gulab jamun'*). He said – "First, have the sweets and celebrate. This time the problem is solved for sure – no mistake about it."

After the boys ate the sweets and had a sip of water from their bottles, Mohinder seated the kids on either side of him on the bench and started speaking.

"Our last pieces of information yesterday - of the theft of flowers, the garland of flowers appearing again on Shanthi's hair, and the changes of duty of the Security Guards – solved the problem for us. All the pieces of the puzzle fit together in my mind. I realized there was an important link between the Guard Santosh and the girl Shanthi apart from them being brother and sister. I now only had to collect the proof regarding my theory.

So, yesterday evening, I made a definite plan. First, I collected the latest tiny Sony camera from my son. The camera can capture photos and video even in dim light. Next, with great effort I woke up at five in the morning – you know I am usually a late riser. I went with my camera and hid behind a bushy plant near the flower bed and waited for things to happen. Fortunately, I had applied some mosquito-repellant cream on my body – so I was safe from being thoroughly bitten.

After about ten minutes, as expected, Santosh walked up the street and halted near the flower bed. He looked in both directions to make sure that nobody was watching him. He did not notice me crouching behind the plant – perhaps he never suspected that somebody would be hiding there to catch him in his act. As he took out a plastic bag from his pocket, I switched on my camera and recorded what he was doing.

Santosh plucked the flowers very quickly with a practiced hand and filled up the bag. Again, he looked all around him and made sure that nobody was watching him. Then he quickly walked on and entered the basement parking area below Block B where his sister Shanthi worked. He hid the plastic bag behind the parked car of Shanthi's employer. Both of them knew that Kimaya's father only left for work around ten in the morning. After this, Santosh left the basement and went back to his guard duty.

I had recorded the video of his hiding the plastic bag as well.

Next, I stood a little away from the entry gate to the Complex and waited for Shanthi's arrival for work that morning. She came in at six O'clock. Unknown to her, I took her photo in my camera. There were no flowers in her hair then. As she went to Kimaya's apartment for work, I went into the basement and waited. I knew she would come there shortly.

Shanthi came to the basement at around seven fifteen and quickly went to the place where the plastic bag with the flowers was kept hidden. She took out a reel of thread and a needle from inside her little purse. She was already ready with the thread inserted into the eye of the needle and so did not have to waste time. Very quickly she made a big garland with all the flowers and stuck it on her hair. She put the plastic bag, the thread and the needle back into her purse and prepared to leave. The whole process took her just about ten minutes or so. Unknown to her, I recorded all of this on my camera.

My mission now accomplished, I went home, had my bath and breakfast and lay down and rested for a while. My back was already hurting."

Tejas and Shreyas were listening breathlessly. This sounded like a spy movie. Tejas's eager question came next – "Then what happened, Uncle?"

Mohinder took a sip of water - his throat was a little dry after the long narration. He resumed after a little pause – "After about an hour's rest, I went to the Estate Manager's Office and called the Security in-charge to join us there. After he came, I showed them the video I had taken on my camera. The proof of guilt of Santosh and Shanthi was so solid that there was no chance of doubt or denial by any of them."

Shreyas asked – "Mohinder Uncle, will they punish the Santosh Uncle and Shanthi Aunty?"

Mohinder sighed – "That is for the Estate Manager and the Security in-charge to do. It is indeed an unpleasant task for them, but has to be done in the greater interest of all the residents. All I know is that the two were called urgently to the Estate Manager's Office in the afternoon today. I can tell you tomorrow once I have a chance to talk to them about what actions they have taken."

The boys went to their game with mixed feelings; happy that the problem had been solved, but sad at the same time because of the impending punishment for the two people involved.

Shreyas the Compassionate

In their apartment later in the evening, Shreyas asked Tejas – "*Dada*, what will they do to Shanthi aunty? My friend Kimaya likes her very much."

Tejas said – "That is for the security to decide, but they had done something wrong and certainly would be punished."

Shreyas had another question for his elder brother – "But why was she making a garland and putting in her hair with those flowers? She could have taken those in the bag itself!"

Tejas was more knowledgeable in such matters, and said – "The security guards at the gate don't allow the maid servants to carry anything out of the Complex without a chit from the owners. But nobody would question a garland in the hair of a woman."

Later in the evening of the next day, they met Mohinder Uncle again. Shreyas asked the question which had been eating him since the previous evening – "What punishment has been given to them, Uncle?"

Mohinder was a little hesitant in communicating the decision taken by the adults to these small children, but went ahead nevertheless – "I told you yesterday that some unpleasant decisions had to be taken. Santosh has been dismissed from service, but Shanthi had been let off lightly – her entry pass to this Complex has been cancelled. She has to find work in other Apartment Complexes nearby. But there is so much demand for domestic helps these days that she should have no difficulty in getting another job – perhaps at a higher salary also."

Shreyas felt bad for Santosh, and said – "Why did Santosh Uncle lose his job, Mohinder Uncle? Shanthi Aunty was not punished so badly!"

Mohinder understood the compassion in the little child's mind. He put his right arm around Shreyas's shoulder and said – "These are things you will learn when you grow up, Shreyas. You see, Santosh was employed as a Security Guard to protect the properties in this Complex, but he dishonoured that trust by stealing things he was supposed to protect. No Security Officer can trust such a person again, so, he had to go. Shanthi's crime was less severe as she only helped in disposing off the stolen flowers, so, she got less punishment."

Shreyas nodded but still had a question – "So, what will Santosh Uncle do now? How will he earn money?"

Mohinder said with a smile now – "That is not a big problem. There are so many big buildings coming up in Bengaluru, that he can get a job in any of them. But he cannot give any reference to his employment here, that's all."

Tejas asked – "But what was Shanthi Aunty doing with so many flowers in her hair every day?"

Mohinder said – "Simply answered – for money, Tejas. Under severe interrogation by the Security Officer, Santosh confessed that once she was out of the gate, Shanthi would go to the Mangammapalya market nearby and sell the garland for some money. That was the game those two played regularly."

Shreyas said – "Now I understand why for one week sometimes there was no stealing of flowers and Shanthi Aunty was without any flower on her hair. That was when Santosh Uncle was not on duty during the night."

Mohinder was pleased that these young kids never failed to amaze him with their intelligence;, and said – "But you kids have done wonderfully well. But for your observation of flowers on Shanthi's hair, we could never have solved 'The Case of the Plucked Flowers'."

All of them did 'high five's as the football mates watched amusedly from a distance.

7. An Eventful Summer (Part 1)

The Good News

It was summer time again – good in some respects, and boring in some. Among the good things were - not having to get up early in the morning to get ready for school in a mad rush (and the inevitable scolding from *Mamma* and *Baba* to hurry and not miss the school bus), plenty of time to play indoor cricket, reading a lot of story books, the weekday summer camps, etc. But sometimes time hung heavily on them – after all, how many books could you read, or how many games could you play just between the two brothers? In the scorching heat outside, it was impossible to go out and play games with friends.

The two Joshi brothers – Tejas the elder and Shreyas the younger, were now nine and six-and-a-half respectively. Both were very intelligent and hyper-active, though they were of different natures. Tejas was very content to sit down and immerse himself in a book when he was not doing anything more serious (a trait he acquired from *Mamma*). He was a very logical kid who would like to have clear and logically correct answers to his questions. Shreyas on the other hand was swayed by feelings and emotions rather than logic and reason; he was very innovative in his approach to problem-solving.

"Kids, *Dadu* and *Nimma* are coming to Bengaluru tomorrow evening." *Mamma* announced one night at the dinner table.

Tejas, as usual, asked his logical question – "From Hyderabad?"

Shreyas quipped – "Don't ask silly questions, *Dada*. We know *Dadu* and *Nimma* stay in Hyderabad. But *Mamma*, I hope *Dadu* is coming with lots of stories to tell us?"

Dadu was *Mamma's* father, and *Nimma* her mother. *Dadu* was in the habit of writing stories, which he would narrate to them at bedtime as a nightly ritual, during their stay in Bengaluru. *Nimma* knew a lot about mythology and Shreyas, being fascinated by all religious characters of late, loved her stories. She would be grilled with probing questions about the

Gods and Goddesses from the younger grandson.

Tejas was more interested in another thing – "*Dadu* can play cricket with me in the house." Tejas was obsessed with cricket at present, and *Dadu* himself having been a good cricketer in his younger days, was always ready to teach a trick or two to his grandsons.

"So kids, surprise *Dadu* and *Nimma* with something when they arrive at our house. Tejas, why don't you write a small story on your own and Shreyas, you can draw a nice picture of Krishna about '*Dahi Handi*'."

"And *Nimma's* name is also Krishna, isn't it *Mamma*?" Shreyas always found it amusing that his two favourites shared the same name.

So, the two boys set about creating their surprise items for their soon-to-arrive grandparents.

Even though the next day was a working day, *Mamma* and *Baba* had gone to their workplace earlier in the morning than usual, so that they could come home a little early to receive the grandparents. But it was well past the expected time and *Mamma*, one who was habitually worried about things not going as per expectations, called *Dadu* on his mobile phone.

"Where are you?" – She asked.

-"…"

"Is it that bad today?"

-"…."

"OK, it may take another hour at least from there."

-"….."

"Please give me a call when you reach Jakkasandra. I can get the tea going so that you can get a hot cuppa when you arrive."

-"…."

"Ok, see you." With that, *Mamma* hung up.

"What happened? Where are they?" *Baba* asked.

Mamma said with a laugh – "*Baba-Ma* are getting a taste of our Bengaluru traffic. They are stuck near Raj Bhavan. The traffic is horrible, it seems."

All of a sudden Shreyas, who was trying to put together some contraptions, got up and stood before his mother with his tiny hands on his hips – "You are laughing? Your parents are stuck in traffic, and you are laughing?"

It was so sudden and so unexpected, that at first everybody looked on in stunned silence and then burst out laughing at this reaction from The Boy Wonder (that's what Shreyas was called because of his clever wit).

Not to be outdone, Tejas lifted his eyes from the book he was reading, and quipped – "As a punishment, you will get caught in a similar traffic jam."

Well, the grandparents finally arrived an hour-and-a-half later. Tea was ready and all of them enjoyed the hot cups of tea with *samosas* and *jalebis*, which *Baba* had bought while returning from the office.

After some conversation, *Dadu* wanted to show to everybody something he had brought from Hyderabad and went into the room where the luggage was kept, and the others continued chatting.

Suddenly there was a high-pitched blood-curdling laughter, and then a yell and the sound of a heavy fall from the room *Dadu* had entered.

"Uhh *Ma*! Uh....Uh...." - obviously, *Dadu* was awfully scared and hurting from the pain as a result of the fall. Everybody went rushing to see the cause and consequence of it all.

Dadu was on the floor on his back with an anguished face and was staring at an object with wide scare-filled eyes.

Mamma was the first to reach her father – "What happened, *Baba?*"

With one hand holding his painful backside, he pointed with the other at the object which caused all this grief – "What....what is that thing? It started laughing at me in such a scary way!"

The 'scary' object was a severe-looking face mask, not a thin one but somewhat thick to accommodate some electronic parts and batteries. Normally, it seemed like a harmless mask, but once moved slightly, it first started a terrible shrieking laughter and the whole face lit up in multiple colours, the scariest one being the flashing blood-red eyeballs. It automatically stopped after a few seconds till moved again. It had a switch at the back to turn it on or off.

It seemed that *Dadu*, being curious to see the mask when his gaze had fallen on it, had picked it up to examine and then all went scarily loose (perhaps the kids had left the switch in the 'on' position). Fortunately, he had fallen on the fleshiest part of his backside, and no mishap happened except for some slight discomfort.

Tejas volunteered – "*Dadu*, we got it from Hong Kong last year during our trip. I found it scary, but Shreyas was so fascinated, he insisted on buying it. I don't know why he did that."

Soon, the culprit was switched off, and everybody got busy to see what 'goodies' *Dadu* and *Nimma* had got for them from Hyderabad.

More Good News

The next fifteen days passed off very well for the Joshi kids. There were a couple of good hours spent on indoor cricket with *Dadu* during which Tejas in particular could get some useful tips about the proper stance while batting and the importance of technique and rhythm while bowling. Afterwards Tejas would busy himself with the books *Dadu* had bought for the kids and Shreyas would park himself with *Nimma* listening to the stories about religious characters, particularly Krishna. In the evening, *Dadu* would help the kids with their summer educational tasks and at bedtime, would tell them stories based on things he had read somewhere, but mostly made up in his mind.

Soon, it was time for the grandparents to return to Hyderabad. But the association was far from over. Unknown to the kids, the elders had plotted a conspiracy to spring a surprise on the kids.

For quite some time, *Dadu* and *Nimma* had been urging *Mamma* and *Baba* to send the kids to Hyderabad to spend some time by themselves with the grandparents, but the parents were hesitating since the kids were not so grown up and they did not want to burden their aging parents with the day-to-day task of looking after two hyper-active children. But now that Tejas and Shreyas had learnt to self-manage, they agreed for a 10-day trip to Hyderabad and accordingly booked train tickets for four (the grandparents and the grandchildren) from Bengaluru to Hyderabad. The arrangement was that *Mamma* and *Baba* would drive down in their car from Bengaluru to Hyderabad after ten days to bring the kids back.

Two days before the scheduled date of journey, *Mamma* broke the secret to the kids – "Children, you two are going to Hyderabad with *Dadu* and *Nimma*. Decide what all you want to take along. I shall then see how much can be packed into your suitcase."

They yelled their pleasure - "Yay! Are we all not going together?"

"No, you two are going with *Dadu* and *Nimma*. We shall come ten days later to get you back. Till then, be my darlings and don't trouble them like you do to us. You know *Dadu* and *Nimma* are quite old."

The children were feeling a little sorry to be away from their parents and *Ajji*, but at the same time thrilled with the prospect of spending more time with *Dadu* and *Nimma* – which meant more stories and play. They were also getting bored with the same old set-up of Bengaluru. A trip to Hyderabad would be a welcome change. Both Tejas and Shreyas were also very fond of *'biryani'* and fish – which they could have in plenty in *Dadu-Nimma's* house. *Dadu* prided himself on being a good cook of the famous Hyderabadi dish.

Soon the kids started selecting their clothes, books and toys which they wanted to carry to Hyderabad. All favourite T-shirts were selected. Tejas wanted to take the iPad and Shreyas wanted to take a few drawing books along with the pencils and colours. When *Mamma* saw the mountain of items to be packed, she firmly told – "Kids, do you think you are going there for good to take so many things? It's only ten days – so take only what you can manage in a single bag for both of you. Apart from that, you can each take a small backpack which you can carry on your back." Having issued the final decree, she proceeded to sort out things which could be accommodated in a single bag.

At the dinner table that night, there was some talk about the nitty-gritties of the journey –food to carry, precautions to be observed, how to keep the two bubbling kids in control on the train, etc. Though the boys were fond of chips and other junk food, *Baba* made it a point to get some less harmful snacks for the round-the-clock-hungry boys. The parents were justifiably a little worried. This was the first time the kids would spend a few days away from their vigilant eyes.

Finally, the talk came around to the safety of their luggage in the train. *Dadu* said that since they came to Bengaluru by air, they had not not carried any safety chains. But that would be necessary as a safety precaution on their return train journey.

"Don't worry. These things are available in the Railway Station. I shall buy three chains when I come to the station to see you off" – said *Baba* reassuringly.

"And I shall prepare some dry dinner items for you all, so you don't have to take the food they serve on the train. After all, you are reaching Hyderabad early next morning anyway" – said *Ajji*.

"Tejas and Shreyas, always be with *Dadu-Nimma* in the train. Don't loiter around. You have no idea what kind of problems can crop up!" This caution was prompted by *Baba*.

The boys nodded dutifully (which they always did whenever issued instructions, but then did things as per their will anyway).

Planning for the Trip

When the boys went to bed later that night, Shreyas asked his elder sibling – "*Dada*, what were they saying about chains at the dinner table? I don't understand why chains are necessary in the train?"

During the discussion at the dinner table, Tejas had been quite absorbed in his meal, and did not hear anything about the chains, but he did not want to admit this to his younger brother and said – "Maybe to tie us down in the train so that we don't go here and there and get lost. They were telling us about sticking to *Dadu-Nimma* in the train. They may not be sure that we shall obey their instructions."

Shreyas thought for a while – "You mean like they take dogs and cats along? No *Dada*, it can't be so. You are making fun of me!"

Tejas smiled in the darkness – "We can ask *Dadu* tomorrow after *Baba* and *Mamma* go to office, to be sure about it."

Soon both fell asleep, dreaming about their train journey.

Next morning, Shreyas asked *Dadu* – "*Dadu*, why do you need chains for our train journey?"

"To make sure that somebody else does not take away our luggage while we are sleeping during the night."

"I don't understand. How will the chain help?"

"You see, we tie our bags with the chain which would be attached to a ring with a lock that is attached to the seats of the train. That way one cannot just take away our bags, without breaking the lock or the chain."

"So, after locking, we can sleep without worrying about the luggage?"

Dadu shook his head slowly and said gravely – "Shreyas, these thieves are quite clever. They know that people put a chain and a lock – so they also come prepared with heavy tools with which they can break the lock or the chain."

"Then what is the use of putting a chain and a lock, *Dadu*? They can still take away our bags!"

Dadu smiled faintly – "We cannot fully make sure that bags are not stolen, but it makes their job that much harder. Also, not all thieves are prepared with heavy tools. Some of them come for a quick steal and run away quickly with whatever they can lay their hands on. Breaking the lock or chain also makes some noise and that sometimes wakes up the passenger. So, it protects your belongings to some extent."

"Can *Dada* and I remain awake during the night one by one to keep watch on our bags, *Dadu?*"

Dadu smilingly hugged Shreyas – "That won't be necessary, darling. It is not that bags are being stolen every day, but the odd chance is always there."

Shreyas nodded and asked – "Have you ever lost anything in the train, *Dadu?*"

Dadu slowly nodded and said – "Yes, a long time back it happened between Calcutta and Kharagpur, where I used to study. I shall tell you about it some other day."

"But in the darkness, how do these thieves know which bag to steal?"

Dadu said – "You see, these thieves work in gangs. Some of them will walk up and down the compartment earlier on some pretext or the other and notice which luggage would be easier to pick and run. Usually, they target the luggage kept closer to the compartment door so that they can quickly jump out if the train is moving slowly, or throw the luggage out if the train is moving fast. They then pull the alarm chain and get out as the train comes to a stop and pick up the bag."

Tejas had joined in the meantime and he now said – "Don't worry, *Dadu*! Both of us will keep watch and look for suspicious characters who walk around inside our compartment."

Dadu was amused and ruffled the hair of the grandsons. It would be fun to travel with these two entertaining kids!

The boys were back in their room, tidying up their toys and other playthings before their journey in the evening.

Tejas said – "Shreyas, why did you tell *Dadu* that we could keep awake at night to watch our luggage? You know that both of us fall asleep immediately when we lie down in the bed!"

Shreyas said seriously – "I had to say something to give some support to *Dadu*. He is an old man and surely cannot keep awake and *Nimma* sleeps deeply as well.".

Tejas pulled himself together and said – "But Shreyas, we have to 'really' do something to help *Dadu*. It would look very bad if our bags are stolen while we are travelling under *Dadu-Nimma's* care."

Shreyas's face showed concern – "Yes, you are right, *Dada*. Let us think of something we can do ourselves."

So, they talked for some time and considered some possibilities. In the end, they agreed on something that would serve the purpose. As they were arranging things in their backpacks, both the brothers slipped an item each into their respective bags. They felt satisfied that now their luggage would be safe.

The Train Journey

The train to Hyderabad was due for departure at six in the evening. *Baba* and *Mamma* returned early from their office at three in the afternoon and after making sure that they had taken care of every necessity for the train journey, they started in their car for the city station at four p.m. They were at the designated platform at approximately five fifteen. *Baba* always believed that it was better to wait leisurely at the station for the train by starting early, rather than being under stress by starting late from the house.

Both Tejas and Shreyas were thrilled as it was their first major train journey with having to sleep overnight in the moving train (their earlier experience was a travel from Bengaluru to Chennai – a day journey, about which they had very little recollection). They were awed by the number of people hurrying about on the platforms and pathways, as if they were about to miss their trains. So many items were available on the platforms – foods, books and magazines, toys and what not! *Baba* located a small shop selling all kinds of items and purchased three steel chains along with locks as they had discussed earlier. Shreyas looked at the strong-looking chains – 'how could the thieves break these strong chains?' – he thought.

As they boarded the AC 2-Tier A-1 coach of the Hyderabad Express, to their dismay they found that their allocated four berths were very close to the door of the compartment. Tejas and Shreyas both remembered what *Dadu* had told them earlier in the morning – that the luggages in this area were the most vulnerable for theft. They exchanged glances with each other but now they did not feel scared as they knew what they themselves could do to prevent such a mishap from happening.

After a round of coffee for the seniors and ice cream for the kids, it was close to the departure time for the train. *Baba* and *Mamma* got down on the platform, but stood close to the window so that they could get the glimpse of the family as long as possible before the train was far out on the platform. *Mamma's* face was somber (she had never before been away from the younger kid for days together), and so was Shreyas's face. Tejas was by now fairly matured to adjust to the reality, so there was no such emotional display from him.

The whistle was blown by the guard at the rear of the train and immediately it was on its way out of the platform. Both the kids kept looking through the stained window to catch sight of their parents as long as possible. Soon, they lost sight of each other as the train gathered speed and chugged out of the platform.

The kids took their iPad out and started playing video games. *Dadu* and *Nimma* kept up a conversation between themselves, planning on how to make the stay of their dear grandchildren in Hyderabad a memorable one.

While playing games, Tejas whispered to his younger brother – "Shreyas, keep observing the suspicious characters that are looking at the luggage as they are walking by repeatedly."

"Yes, *Dada*, I have already spotted a red-shirted person who was trying to spot the luggage under our seats. He certainly looks suspicious to me."

"I have also seen a person wearing a black T-shirt who kept looking at both sides as if to plan where to strike during the night."

They were excited that they had been able to spot the culprits even before they could get a chance to commit any offence.

The four of them had their dinner at eight. *Ajji* had prepared soft *rotis* and *paneer* curry for the journey and *Baba* had bought some *sandesh*– it was quite adequate for all. At nine, *Dadu* made the bed for all and asked the kids to sleep. Tejas and Dadu occupied the upper berths, and Shreyas and *Nimma* took the lower ones (*Nimma* being arthritic, could not climbup. Shreyas was still too young, and for his safety while sleeping, he was assigned a lower berth).

As the lights were put out and *Dadu* went up, Shreyas waited for the sound of *Dadu's* snoring. Then he quietly took two things out of his and Tejas's backpacks. One of them he kept on the suitcase nearest to the passage, and the other object he kept holding in his hand as slowly he fell asleep.

The Trap Comes Alive

As all the passengers in the darkened compartment were deep in sleep a few hours later, all of a sudden, a blood-curdling piercing laughter, enough to scare the most courageous to death, shattered the silence. Simultaneously, a frightened-to-death yell came through – "AAAAANNNN......, AMMAAAAA...., *bachao, bachao.*". Everybody sprang up in their bed, and climbed down to enquire what was happening. Scurrying to the spot of the incident, the passengers found a red-shirted young man shivering with fright, and holding his head in pain.

It was the Chinese scary mask in play, as planted by Shreyas on the suitcase. As the thief tried to remove the luggage, the mask got activated and let out that unworldly scary laughter along with the frighteningly flashing red eyeballs and all kinds of colours flashing on that ghastly mask-face. It was so scary in the dark that the young man sprang backwards and fell on his back, only to hurt himself. Just then Shreyas woke up and hit the fellow on the head with the short stout stick he had held in his hand at the time of going to sleep. The poor thief got much more than he ever feared.

The other accomplice (the black T-shirted youth) was waiting near the door to collect the loot and slip down. As the pandemonium prevailed in the compartment, he forgot himself and jumped from the train without realizing that the train was moving too fast to do that. In the process, he broke his leg as he hit the ground and was later captured by the Railway Police.

A few interested passengers came to enquire how it all started. *Dadu* told them about the mask and the clever trap set by his grandsons. Before the passengers got off in the morning when the train arrived at the Kacheguda Station in Hyderabad, everybody had come to know about the feat of the Joshi brothers. All smilingly congratulated the boys and wished them luck in life.

Tejas and Shreyas did 'High Fives' to celebrate the success of their plan. Tejas told *Dadu* – "Now I am glad that Shreyas had purchased that mask in Hong Kong."

The matter was brought to the notice of Railway Police through the guard of the train who also took down *Dadu's* address and phone number in Hyderabad, promising to get a citation for the kids for the good deed on their part – because of which two notorious luggage-lifters had been caught.

An Eventful Summer

(Part 2)

Vacation in Hyderabad

Tejas and Shreyas spent an enjoyable time in Hyderabad in the company of *Dadu* and *Nimma*. *Dadu* made it a point to wake the boys up a little early in the morning, and go for a walk along the Old Airport Road (OAR), which had no traffic in the early hours. During these walking trips, he explained about all the visible landmarks around. There were some interesting old incidents as well, which he narrated to the fascinated kids. One such story was very interesting.

The Begumpet airport was just astride the OAR and the boys could see some small planes taking off and landing at close range. Through some small slit openings on the boundary wall, they could see the take-off and landings very clearly. The City Airport for regular commercial flights had been shifted to far-away Shamshabad. As a consequence, the one at Begumpet was now being used for training and some VIP flights. *Dadu* said that in the month of February, this Airport usually hosted an International Air Show when many huge planes like Airbus-380 were put on public display. During that period of three days, acrobatic exercises by skilled team of fliers could be seen by residents around this area. The kids were very interested and expressed the desire to come again in February to see the acrobatic exercises.

Dadu said that when he had come to Hyderabad for the first time 38 years ago in the 1970's, Begumpet was the only Airport. *Dadu's* place of work was located just on the other side of the Airport Runway and at that time, if there was no flight (anyway there were not many flights those days), all vehicles were allowed to cross the runway and crossover from one side of the Airport to the other side very quickly. It saved a lot of time and travel since otherwise one had to go all the way around the Airport to cross from one side to the other.

It so happened that one day the gatekeeper who opened the gates to allow vehicles to cross, did not notice that a flight was about to land. It was very dangerous because if an airplane landing at high speed happened to hit a vehicle on the ground, it would be disastrous for both. To make matters worse, there was a high official of the Government of India on the flight and he happened to see vehicles on the runway just as the plane was about to land. Rightly, he was furious and put a stop to any vehicle crossing the runway at any time of the day, once and for all.

There was another scary incident about which *Dadu* told the boys and later on showed the boys exactly where it had happened. About five years ago, one of the airplanes taking part in the acrobatics during the Air Show lost control over the plane and crashed into a house hardly 100 metres from *Dadu's* house. He was in the kitchen when he heard a deafening sound and came out to find the source, only to find people running towards the crash site nearby. Unfortunately, the two pilots in the plane died on the crash site, though there was no other casualty on the ground. The house on which the plane fell was extensively damaged. It could have been *Dadu's* house also (being so close) if bad luck had prevailed.

Life otherwise was enjoyable for the kids. Both were very fond of eating fish and so *Dadu* took them along every day to buy fresh fish from a nearby shop. The boys could see different varieties and in the shop pointed to the one they wanted to eat that day.

There were stories aplenty for the boys from *Dadu* and *Nimma* every day. During the daytime *Dadu* made sure that the boys did some of the work assigned for the summer vacation in preparation for the next session at school.

The boys were delighted to be treated to some excellent dishes which they had never had before. *Nimma* always had an excellent touch in cooking and she prepared some special items lovingly for her dear grandsons. Two items in particular were her signature dishes – *Bagara* Rice and Cabbage *Payasam* (nobody could make out that the outstanding dessert could be made from the lowly cabbage). Since the boys were fond of fish, she also prepared some special fish curries.

An Undesirable Irritant

Dadu was past seventy and he usually felt the need for a short nap in the afternoon. Since it was summer, the hot weather made it all the more necessary.

A few days after Tejas and Shreyas had come to Hyderabad, *Dadu* was taking a nap in the afternoon and the boys were engaged in some tasks *Dadu* had given them. Suddenly, the door-bell rang to shatter the silence in the house. *Dadu* woke up and went outside to see who had come to the gate, but couldn't find anyone at the gate. In an irritated mood (who would like to be disturbed like this for no reason, while taking a nap?), he came back into the house grumbling – "Oh, those mischief-makers again!"

Tejas asked – "Who was it, *Dadu*?"

"There are some young boys in our neighbourhood who keep disturbing us like this frequently!"

"Who are they, *Dadu*? Why don't you catch them?"

Dadu's irritation showed on his face – "They are a few boys from that street nearby. I have a hunch who the culprits are, but unfortunately I have never been able to catch them in the act."

"Why, *Dadu*?"

"They just ring the bell and run away. By the time I come out to see, those boys had vanished."

"Can you not switch off the bell while you are sleeping?"

"I do sometimes, but don't remember all the time. Moreover, there are genuine callers like the courier man, the Postman, other visitors etc. If I keep the bell switched off, they will go away thinking nobody is at home."

Tejas started thinking and after some time said – "But *Dadu*, if you know those boys in the next street, can you not talk to their parents?"

Dadu shook his head – "I did, to a couple of households with the assumption that the boys from those households were the mischief-makers, but the parents dismissed the suggestion claiming that their boys could not do such a thing."

Tejas instantly said – "Somehow we have to prove to them."

That night in bed, the boys were still concerned about this problem and started discussing it.

Shreyas said – "*Dada*, if I get God's eyes, I can see what happened earlier."

Tejas knew his brother was obsessed with Gods and their super-powers. He was the one with a logical mind and wanted down-to-earth reasons. He said – "Shreyas, for that you don't have to have God's abilities. I can tell you how we can do that."

"How?"

"When we take part in a music programme, we cannot see our own performance in the Hall because we are on the stage. But *Baba* shows us later how we had performed – right?"

Shreyas got the idea – "Yes, *Baba* shows us the video."

Tejas sat up in the bed – "That's the idea – we have to take the video of those boys doing the mischief."

"But do you know how to take video, *Dada?*"

"Yes, *Baba* had let me try taking photos and videos sometimes, so I know how to take them. And you know Shreyas, *Baba* and *Dadu* both have the same mobile phones – Moto X Play! That makes the job easy. Good, man! We found a solution to *Dadu's* problem now."

"But how will you take the video? *Dadu* said that by the time he comes out on hearing the bell, those boys vanish."

Tejas was already thinking – "I don't know yet, but shall find a way. Let us discuss with *Dadu* tomorrow morning. Let's go to sleep now"

Tejas excitedly revealed his scheme to *Dadu* next morning. *Dadu* was pleasantly surprised that these two young kids were concerned about his problem and had already worked out a plan. But he said – "Don't bother about it, my dears! I think the problem will go away once these boys grow up a little and realize their mistake."

"No *Dadu*! Let us stop this now so that you don't have to suffer every day. Please tell me, can we stand in that street corner and take video to catch them in their act?" They were standing near the gate when this conversation was going on.

"Oh no, Tejas! It is peak summer and you will get a heatstroke if you stand in the afternoon sun out in the open."

Tejas looked around and his face lit up – "*Dadu*, there it is! I can sit in your opposite neighbour's first-floor balcony and take video through the openings in the wall, and *Dadu*, there is no sun there, it is covered." He pointed at the first-floor balcony of the house right opposite to theirs - across the street.

Dadu was amazed. The young kid had thoughts running in the right direction; and the approach was a viable one too!

Tejas added further – "I can have a clear view not only of the gate, but also a lot of the street on both sides. So, I can see them approaching, in the act and while escaping. If I can take a video of all that, then you will have your proof."

Dadu was hesitant, but felt that the enthusiasm of the children should not be snuffed out altogether. He said – "Alright, let's try it today for one day only. I do not want you to spend the hot afternoon in the balcony too often. But before we sit down and plan how we proceed, I have to do one important thing."

Shreyas asked – "What is it, *Dadu*?"

"I have to talk to my friend and neighbor Narasimha Rao."

"Who is he?"

"He is the owner of the opposite house. If you are going to wait and watch from his balcony, I have to take his permission first, isn't it?"

Both the kids nodded. "Let's go right now and talk to him. Kids, you can also come with me." - said *Dadu*.

The three of them walked across the street and called on Rao. He was also as old as *Dadu* and very jovial. He had watched *Mamma* grow up from her own kid days and was very happy to see her delightful sons now. He was overjoyed when he came to know about the plan and patted the boys on the back for their wonderful adventurous spirit.

"What can I do to make your plan a success? Should I also wait in the balcony with you?" – asked Rao.

Dadu said -"No, Rao *Garu* (form of respect in Telugu). If you are seen on the balcony along with the kids, those boys will smell a rat and will not commit their act. But you can do one thing – without being seen, you can watch the scene. You have been staying here much longer than me and so may be able to recognize them better than me. Later on, we can confront their parents."

"Done! I shall watch through a slight opening in the window but stay inside the room like Meghnad – see everything, but remain unseen" – said Rao with a laugh.

Dadu came back to his house with Tejas and Shreyas.

Having agreed on their surveillance plan for the afternoon, the three of them sat down to finalize the detailed plan. The first thing *Dadu* ensured was to confirm that Tejas knew how to take video recording on the Moto X Play mobile phone.

The Moment Comes

From his past experience, *Dadu* knew that the boys appeared between three-thirty and four

O'clock in the afternoon whenever they pressed the switch for the door-bell. So, at around three-fifteen, he escorted Tejas and Shreyas to the balcony of Rao's house. Rao himself sat inside the room with the window curtain kept slightly open to have a clear view. *Dadu* came back to his house and waited inside the car parked in the portico. He had decided to forego his regular afternoon nap that day as he was also equally excited about the plan.

Tejas instructed – "Shreyas, you keep a watch on both sides of the street and alert me so that I can be ready with the mobile for the video recording when they come to press the door-bell switch. But don't shout, just a whisper will do."

Shreyas nodded. He knew the importance of keeping silent.

Half an hour passed without anything happening. Would those boys give a go by today? Anyway, there was still time. But around four O'clock, Shreyas's vigilant eyes saw three boys entering the street from the left side. From the way they looked at the houses on each side of the street and approached the gates of some, it was quite clear to Shreyas that those indeed were the culprits. *"Dada!"*- He said in a hushed whisper.

Tejas immediately got busy on the mobile and got the video recording going. *Dadu* from inside his car had a clear view of the balcony. Shreyas gave him a thumbs-up signal which was reciprocated by his grandfather. All was set!

Unmindful of the trap for capturing evidence, the three young boys (all in the range of ten to twelve years of age) crept up to the gate and pressed the switch for the door-bell as they had been doing for so many days in the past. *Dadu* was immediately out of the car seat and shouting at them. Taken aback, the boys started running. Rao also came out of his room and stood on the balcony along with Tejas and Shreyas to get a clearer view. In a matter of a few seconds, the boys had run around the corner of the street and were out of sight. The entire incident was very skilfully recorded by Tejas on the video.

Rao came down from the first floor along with the kids and all met at the gate of *Dadu's* house. *Dadu* asked – "Rao *Garu*, could you recognize those three boys?"

"I have some idea, but would like to see the video to be sure."

They all came inside the house and Tejas played the video recording to Rao *Garu* who, after closely observing, said – "Yes, I am sure now. The boy in the yellow T-shirt is Sai Gopal, the one in blue is Pravin and the third in red is a boy whose name I don't know, but his father has that pan shop around this corner."

Dadu patted Tejas and Shreyas on the back and said – "Well done, boys! Now go and relax for some time. I have kept some ice-cream for you as the reward for the good work done, but since you have just come in from the hot sun outside, I shall give you the ice-cream a little later. Let me talk to Rao *Garu* about how to take the matter up with the families of those boys."

Rao volunteered to come with *Dadu* to talk with the parents (*Dadu* was not so familiar with the local language Telugu and Rao's presence solved that problem). At first, the parents were adamant that their children could not do such mischief; but once they were shown the video replay, they had no further defence for their wards. They apologetically promised to take their wards to task to ensure that such acts were not repeated in future.

Dadu did not face this problem in future again, thanks to the initiative by Tejas and Shreyas.

8. Not Sherlock's Day

Preparations for Birthday Celebrations

"So Tejas, how would you like to celebrate your tenth birthday?" asked *Mamma* a few days before the D-Day. The parents always invited suggestions from the kids and avoided total imposition of their own ideas for the kids' significant occasions.

Tejas had already done some thinking regarding this year's celebration; so, he was mostly prepared.

"*Mamma*, last year we went out to play cricket and then had our food in Chef's Bakers. It was a lot of fun, but this year we should do something different."

Baba looked up from what he was doing (in fact, he was listing various possibilities in a pad for the same purpose) and said – "Do you have anything in mind?"

"Yes *Baba*, we can have it in the house itself this time without making it too complicated. Instead of cooking, we can order some Pizzas and Chinese noodles and spend more time on games that we can enjoy."

Baba and *Mamma* exchanged glances – 'These kids are growing up and have started putting their minds to matters. That's a good sign!' – They thought.

"Okay, if that's what you want, let us make a detailed plan. There's hardly a week left until your Birthday. Shreyas, you also come and plan with us."

Tejas and Shreyas were the two Joshi brothers – Shreyas being about two years and a half younger. Both were very intelligent and active children.

The Plan

The five of them (the kids' grandmother, *Ajji* was also part of the planning team) sat down and discussed various possibilities. The kids wanted to include both indoor and outdoor games plus some thinking games which could be conducted within the house. *Mamma* gave some suggestions based on her experience from her student days. After an hour's deliberations, they evolved the following games.

1. French cricket: This was a game taught to the kids by Dadu during his last visit to

Bengaluru. They could play this in front of their G-block building in the ground floor. Tejas' friends had not played this game earlier and so, it would be a unique experience for them. All it required was a bat and a ball and it could be played in a limited area.

2. English Olympiad: Tejas had come first in the State-level International English Olympiad in the previous year and received a gold medal for it. He wanted his friends to get a taste of this exercise. Everybody would get a chance to ask a question and answer others' questions.

3. Dart Throwing: Tejas had a magnetic Dart Board, which could be fixed on the wall and friends could throw magnetic Darts from marked distances. Greater the distance, greater the marks scored.

4. Dumb Charades: This would be played in pairs. Kids would have to pick a chit from a box and silently act out the subject matter based on which his partner had to identify what was written in the chit.

5. Find the Hidden Treasure: One kid had to discover the treasure hidden by the rest of the kids within a limited time and a maximum of ten questions could be asked to which answers would only be 'yes' or 'no'. To make matters simple, the hidden

treasure had to be one from the five objects selected earlier for this game. For example – a bat, a book, a toy, a mobile phone or a biscuit-packet.

All five agreed that it was a good combination of physical and mental games which would keep everybody engaged for half a day at least. *Baba* said he would arrange for ice-cream, fruits and other snacks in addition to the planned pizza and noodles, as the young kids felt hungry all the time.

The list of kids to be invited was also prepared. The list included the two brothers Rajesh and Rakesh, Sunil, Daksh, Vinod, Atharv and the twins, Pranab and Arnab. The twins were identical in looks and manners, and it was virtually impossible for anybody other than their parents to identify them correctly – the only difference being one (Pranab) had glasses and the other did not.

There would be eleven kids in all and that was not a big number to host within the house.

Since Tejas's birthday fell on a Tuesday, it was decided to have the Kids' Party on the preceding Sunday so that all kids could attend. The kids were told to come in some 'theme' costumes if they could, from whatever was available in their respective houses.

Tejas Spills the Beans

On Friday morning, a couple of days before the day of the Party, the kids were waiting at the bus stop for their school bus. Inquisitive friends asked – "So Tejas, what fun are we going to have in your Party?"

Without much thinking, Tejas started babbling – "Many things! But the most exciting would be the game to hunt for the hidden treasure. All of us would be investigating like......." Before he could divulge anything more, Shreyas pinched him and said in a whisper – "*Dada*, don't tell them everything beforehand!" Realizing his mistake, Tejas stopped in his tracks and refused to say anything more.

When Tejas and Shreyas came down to play football in the evening, they found the rest of their group of friends huddled up and discussing something seriously. As the brothers approached, they split up and got the game started.

The Party Begins

At ten on Sunday morning, all the boys came together – or almost. Some of them came in 'theme' dresses as requested earlier. Rajesh and

Rakesh were dressed in *'Vaishnav'* Saint style (saffron-coloured long cloaks). Sunil was dressed as a *Pathan*, Tanmay as a Cowboy (with gun-belt dangling from his waist), and Pranab dressed in typical Assamese style with a colourful short jacket, a *'Toka'* (flat straw hat) adorning his head; he also wore an impressive-looking watch on his wrist. Arnab could not come as he had a slight fever. Tejas and Shreyas were dressed as Maratha warriors. The other kids were in colourful dresses but

not in the 'theme' style. The whole spectacle was so eye-catching and colourful that Baba took photographs of all, first individually and then as a group. The party promised to be thoroughly enjoyable, the only sad note being Arnab's absence. *Baba* and *Mamma* took over the job of directing and keeping the ten kids in control.

To utilize the kids' energy in the best way, the physical and mental games were spaced alternately. The first game was dart throwing. Since darts hitting the target from the farthest distance would fetch more points, the temptation for the young kids was to try to throw from the farthest line. The first round resulted in zero score for everybody. Sensing that the kids needed to be given the right advice, *Baba* explained the principle of striking a balance between marks scored and the chance of success (it was difficult to hit the target from a longer distance). The second round was better for everybody, except for Rajesh who did not heed the advice and kept throwing from the farthest distance. At the end of the game of three rounds, Rakesh (who had kept a cool head) was the winner.

Baba and *Mamma* had arranged for prizes for all winners to be given at the end of the day.

They now switched to a mental game – 'English Olympiad'. Tejas was perhaps the most comfortable in this game since he had done extremely well at the State level. The game started with all the boys sitting in a circle. Each kid had a chance to ask the one to his right the spelling and the meaning of a word. If told correctly, the answer-giver would get points, but if he got it wrong, the question passed to the kid on his right. Anybody giving the correct answer would get the point. If nobody was able to give the correct answer, the question came back to the first kid and he had to tell everybody the right answer. In case he himself did not know the answer to the question he asked, he would get a negative mark. The game went on with *Mamma* being the Referee and the Scorer. Tejas was the runaway winner with Rajesh scoring the second highest.

Now it was time again for a physical game – 'French Cricket'. Everybody went downstairs along with *Baba*. Tejas had done a good thing the day before. Without telling anyone about it being a part of the Party, he had explained about the rules of play at school the previous day. So even though they had not played it earlier, all the children were aware of the game's rules and techniques. Three circles were drawn on the ground. The innermost and smallest was just large enough for one kid to stand with a bat in hand. The second circle was bigger and four fielders (cum throwers) were allowed to stand on the edge of the circle, without entering into the inner space. The other six fielders were on the edge of the outer circle. The throwers on the inner ring would try to hit the legs of the batsman and if successful, the batsman would be out. The batsman on the other hand tried to hit the ball with the bat as far away as possible. If he was able to send the ball beyond the inner ring, he would score a run, and if it crossed the outer ring, that would be a boundary of four runs. The ball hit over the outer ring would be a 'six' and fetch six runs. But if any of the fielders caught the ball hit by the batsman before it touched the ground, the batsman would be out. None of the six fielders on the outer ring could throw the ball directly at the batsman, but had to pass it on to the throwers on the inner ring.

The game was a thrilling one for the kids. There was a gap of five minutes for them to catch their breath. Pranab left the group to go to the basement washroom and joined back rather quickly by the time the game resumed. *Baba* had thoughtfully brought along some bananas and the kids hungrily devoured them to replenish their energy.

Sunil won the game because he was very agile and kept a cool head. Tejas missed the top score by just a single run. Pranab's game went haywire after the short break as he was not able to connect a single ball with his bat and scored the lowest.

The sun was quite warm by this time and the kids were a little tired. Everybody went up again. *Baba* announced that there would be a break now from the games as the food was expected to arrive in five minutes.

Soon, the food arrived, and the boys were ravishingly hungry after the morning's hectic activities. The dishes – Pizza and Chinese noodles with Vegetable Manchurian were their favourite, and everybody did full justice to the meal.

The Games go on

After the heavy meal, the kids were not expected to indulge in physical games immediately, and so a mind game was rightly scheduled – 'Dumb Charades'. Though the game was not totally unfamiliar, they had not played it much earlier.

Mamma had planned in advance. She had scribbled the names, acts etc. on a number of folded chits of paper and put them in a box. The kids formed five teams of two each. One from the team would pick up a chit from the box, read what was written on the paper and through hand/body gestures and eye movements (but no spoken word or lip movement) act in such a manner that his partner could come out with the answer (the partner was allowed to speak) within the allotted time of two minutes. If the correct answer could not be given or the person acting spoke any word or made any sound, the team lost its chance. For example, if the scribbled word was the film 'Jungle Book', then the first kid would try to convey that it was a film by hand movements and eye gestures. The partner then could ask him whether it was a film, to which a simple nod would confirm the same. Then the actor would proceed to convey 'jungle' and then 'book' through gestures. Any verbal query from the partner could be confirmed or declined only through a nod or a shake of the head. Each team would get its chance and after three rounds, the game would conclude.

The team of Tanmay and Atharv won the game at the end with Rajesh and Rakesh coming a close second.

It was almost three O'clock by the time they came to the last and the most challenging game of the day – 'Find the Hidden Treasure', when the little 'Sherlocks' would apply their minds to both hide and to trace articles inside the house.

The game was played like this. One kid (say A) whose turn it was, would be asked to step out of the house for a while. The remaining kids would hide one object out of the five pre-selected ones somewhere inside the house and then ask A to step in and hunt the object down. He could ask a maximum of ten questions and would have to find the object within five minutes. If he could find by asking less number of questions and in less time, then he would get more marks. The winner would be 'The Sherlock Holmes' of the day.

The game turned out to be very interesting, and on popular demand, a second round was also played. Surprisingly, Shreyas emerged as the 'Sherlock Holmes of the Day'. He had shown remarkable intuition about where things could be hidden. He was complimented by the kids, all of whom were elder to him.

The birthday celebrations for Tejas were an outstanding success. Not only was he happy, his friends also felt happy about the 'celebrations with a difference'.

It was now almost five-thirty and time for the kids to go back to their respective houses, but not before being treated to some ice-creams and waffles.

Baba-Mamma gave the prizes to the winners of games (and small gifts to everybody) before the kids left. The elders sat down at the table and kept watching the children with satisfied smiles on their faces – all their efforts had yielded the expected results.

Tejas came hurrying back from the front door with concern on his face – "*Baba*, Pranab can't find his watch."

"What's happened? How is it missing?"

"He kept it on the shelf above the TV when we all went down to play cricket downstairs, and now it is not there!"

With worried faces, *Baba* and *Mamma* went near the front door where the kids were talking among themselves in agitated tones.

"Pranab, are you sure you did not take it with you when you went down to play?" - asked *Baba*.

"No Uncle, I left it on that shelf. I was afraid it might get damaged if I fell down while running around playing cricket."

Rajesh also confirmed – "Yes Uncle, I had also seen him keeping it there."

"What kind of watch was it?"

Pranab looked somewhat down in spirits – "It has a big blue dial, Uncle. My father got it from Singapore last month."

Everybody started searching for the watch in the nearby spaces, but there was no trace of the watch anywhere.

Vinod quipped in the spirit of fun – "Uncle, is it possible that it was hidden as a part of our game?"

Rajesh added – "Then Shreyas the Sherlock has to find it!"

Despite the attempts at humour, the atmosphere was one of concern at the loss of the watch. Tejas had been really happy till the loss was discovered. Even the elders in the house felt that the high spirits of a few minutes ago was missing now.

More searches everywhere, but the result was the same. Then Pranab did something totally unexpected. He stood near the front door and said – "Please don't mind my searching all your pockets before you leave. This is to make sure that nobody blames you later that you walked away with the watch in your pocket. I hope you don't mind."

Everybody was surprised, but nodded their agreement.

The body search was carried out but with no success.

"Tejas, now you search me. Let this be a fair search" – said Pranab.

Tejas carried out the search, but could not find anything. Tejas and Shreyas were earlier searched by Pranab.

With worried faces, the kids left one by one. The elders and the two Joshi boys sat down to discuss the incident and speculating about what had happened.

The Investigation

The seniors looked at each other not knowing how to proceed. Tejas was feeling bad because his friend lost his dear watch during his birthday party. Only Shreyas was surprisingly undisturbed and tried to put on a funny face, as was his wont.

Nimma spoke up – "I think it is our moral duty to replace Pranab's watch because it got lost from right under our noses." *Dadu* and *Nimma* were visiting Bengaluru to celebrate Tejas's tenth birthday at that time.

Mamma said – "Though it's not a big problem, let's find out how it could have happened. Tejas and Shreyas, is it possible that Pranab did not bring his watch at all?"

"No *Mamma*, I saw it very clearly in his hand and helped him put it in a safe place before we all went down. It was a big watch for his hands and it had a blue dial with white pointers."

"And Shreyas, tell us honestly, did you hide it anywhere and not tell anybody?"

Shreyas climbed down from his chair and theatrically folded his hands and said with bowed head – "No, Mother Mary! I did not!"

Mamma looked at *Baba* and said - "Apart from us and the boys, there was nobody else in the house. Razia (their domestic help) was also there, but she would never do such a thing – but wait a minute! The delivery boys were here with the food – could it be one of them?"

Baba dismissed the suggestion – "No chance! They delivered the packages at the front door. I carried them inside after making the payment. Looks like Tejas' safe place --" - his sentence was interrupted by the telephone ringing. He went immediately to receive the call.

As *Baba* was talking on the phone, the others continued speculating about who the culprit could be, but did not get any viable lead into the mystery.

After finishing his telephone conversation, *Baba* came back to the table. He seemed to be in deep thought holding his head in both palms and staring down at the table cloth. After about a minute he looked up. There was a decisive expression on his face as he said – "I think we are too obsessed with it right now. No clue will emerge this way. Let's shift our attention to our regular work and think calmly. That is the only way we can hit upon something we are all missing at this point. But for the time being let us leave this problem to our little Sherlocks here. Tejas and Shreyas, you two had played the detectives' roles in the game today. The time has come to solve a real-life problem."

Tejas asked – "But how do we solve this mystery?"

"Sit down and think calmly. Go over the day's activities in sequence and try to recollect who did what at each point of time. Try to recollect any strange behaviour of any of your friends. Information and observation are the two most effective tools to arrive at the logical deduction for solving any problem in real life."

"Kids, we are tired and we have a lot of cleaning up to do. Since your homework was already done yesterday, go to your room and do as *Baba* said" – *Mamma* said as she got up to attend to the pending work.

Back in their room, Tejas and Shreyas sat on the bed. It was one of those rare occasions when the siblings were not busy with the iPad or their games or fighting noisily. Seriousness was evident on their faces.

"*Dada*, who do you think could have done it?" Shreyas asked after a few moments.

"If we can rule out ourselves, it could have been any of the others". Tejas said but then screwed his eyes and looked at his younger brother – "Shreyas, I hope it is not one of your childish pranks?" Shreyas at seven-and-a-half was still fond of playing childish games sometimes.

In all seriousness Shreyas sat up and said – "No *Dada*! I tell you honestly, it's not me!"

Tejas nodded slightly – "We can rule out Pranab. He won't take his own watch and play out a drama like this. That leaves Rajesh, Rakesh, Vinod, Sunil, Daksh, Atharv and Tanmay. Did you see any of them going near the shelf where the watch was kept?"

"See *Dada*, we played all our games in the living room. Only the dart game was played inside our room. Some of them went out to go to the washroom or for drinking water. If any of them took it at that time, we wouldn't know about it."

"But we searched everybody before they left, so, nobody could have taken it away." Tejas dismissed Shreyas's idea.

"You are right!"- Shreyas said, and as an afterthought he added – "But it could be a prank on us – somebody might have hidden it in our house itself."

Tejas liked this one – "Quite possible! Come on, let's make a thorough search of the whole house."

The boys searched all conceivable places diligently, including the shoe rack and the refrigerator, but it was fruitless. They gave up after an hour.

The kids had the leftovers from the morning food for their dinner. Just before they came to the table, they saw *Baba*, *Mamma* and *Ajji* talking in hushed tones.

The Consultant

The kids were there at the school bus stop next morning. All their friends from the apartment complex were also there including Arnab. He appeared to have recovered from his fever. Naturally, their talk hovered around the fun they had on the previous day as well as the loss of the watch. But one thing struck Tejas – the boys took the incident more as fun than as something to be sorry about. But that was to be expected of kids of their age – he knew that. Unless it directly affected them, kids look at all such things with fun. Only Pranab looked a little subdued – as the one who suffered the loss.

Shreyas observed that Arnab was wearing a watch that looked similar to what Pranab had the previous day – the only difference being that its dial was red in colour. As Shreyas approached him with curiosity and pointed at the watch, Arnab said – "This one is mine, Shreyas. Our father got two watches for us from Singapore. My watch has a red dial, and Pranab's had a blue one."

On their walk from the bus stop back to their house in the evening, Tejas said – "I don't know how to proceed further, Shreyas. Let's ask somebody for help."

Shreyas nodded – "Yes, let us talk to Mohinder Uncle." Mohinder Taneja was the elderly widower ex-army Colonel who was residing in the same complex and had become good friends with Shreyas in particular. Together they had solved a few problems in the past.

A little later in the evening when the boys came to the play area for a game of football, Mohinder Uncle was, as usual, sitting on the stone bench nearby. The Joshi brothers went up and said – "Uncle, after the game we want to discuss some problem with you. Please wait for us."

Mohinder sensed some interesting mystery (he immensely liked to associate with the young minds by taking part in their small adventures), and smilingly ruffled the hair of his favourite kid-friend – "Welcome, dear! I shall be here."

Later on, the three of them sat down together and Tejas narrated the entire incident that took place the previous day. Mohinder listened to the narration, occasionally nodding gently. At the end he asked – "Doesn't Pranab have a twin brother? I see them always together."

"Yes, but Arnab couldn't come for the party since he had fever."

"But just now I saw both of them playing football with you boys!"

"Yes, looks like he has recovered fully."

"Strange! Somebody having viral fever yesterday and missing a kids' party feels strong enough to play football the next day!" He seemed to ponder over the matter for a few seconds before asking – "Now tell me, did any of your friends move away from the group any time?"

Tejas said – "Yes, when we were playing dart throwing inside our room, some of them came out for water or to go to the washroom."

"Anything else?"

Shreyas said – "When we were playing French Cricket downstairs, Pranab rushed to the washroom in the basement, but he came back very quickly."

"French Cricket! What is that game? I have never heard of it."

Tejas was very proud of his familiarity with this new game – "Our *Dadu* from Hyderabad taught us this game. It is very interesting."

Mohinder asked again – "Okay, did you notice any strange behaviour on the part of any of your friends at the party?"

Shreyas responded – "Sunil and Rajesh were exchanging glances very frequently and looking at Pranab and smiling by themselves for no reason. Oh, one more thing! Pranab was having some difficulty in reading the chit during the Dumb Charades game. He had to take out his specs to read clearly."

Mohinder had a grave expression on his face and made a sound like 'Ummm' a few times. Then he asked – "Pranab is the brother who wears glasses, or is it Arnab? I can't tell the difference otherwise."

"Pranab, Uncle."

Mohinder got up – "I am beginning to get a hang of the mystery, but it depends on one answer. You ask your mother a question when you get back home and tell me the answer over telephone immediately. You remember my number, right?"

Shreyas nodded and the two brothers started walking back to their apartment after Mohinder told them what question to ask *Mamma*.

As soon as the kids came back to the house, they went to *Mamma* and asked – "*Mamma*, after we went downstairs to play cricket yesterday, did any of my friends come up to the house before we all came back together?"

Mamma said – "I was in the kitchen for some time arranging the entire cutlery. If anybody had come during that time, I wouldn't know, but I didn't see anybody coming otherwise."

Ajji was sitting nearby, and as she listened to Tejas's question and *Mamma's* answer, she said –"But Pranab came to visit the washroom. He was in a hurry – just ran in and ran out."

"Was he wearing his specs?"

Ajji shook her head – "I did not notice all that closely. I was reading a book."

Shreyas went to the telephone and called a number and spoke for some time.

"Excellent! I shall meet you at the bus stop tomorrow morning and tell you what to do. Reach the bus stop a little early before the other boys come. We are very close to solving the mystery. Unless I am grossly mistaken, the missing watch would be recovered by this evening" - came the reply from the other end.

Mamma was curious about this question, and she asked – "Shreyas, who did you speak to?"

With a mischievous smile Shreyas said – "Our consultant."

Mamma was puzzled – "Consultant! Who is he?"

Shreyas said – "Mohinder Uncle", and ran into the room. The two brothers started talking in low tones thereafter.

Mystery Uncovered

Mohinder was at the bus stop waiting for his little friends. The other boys were yet to come.

Quickly, he explained to the kids what they had to do that evening. "I will be sitting there on the bench watching the fun." He left even before any other boys reached the bus stop.

Shreyas did not join in the game that evening, but stood on the side. He claimed to have a sprain in his foot.

As the game went on, Tejas asked Pranab – "Pranab, can I ask Shreyas to go to your house and get a bottle of water for me? I forgot to bring mine today and I am feeling very thirsty." Pranab's house was right next to the play area and their balcony could be clearly seen.

"Yes, why not? Shreyas, go and tell Mummy to give a bottle of water."

Shreyas walked up to the second-floor apartment of the Dekas and rang the door-bell. Himani Deka, Pranab and Arnab's mother, opened the door.

"Yes Shreyas, do you want something?" She was a very pleasant and simple lady who liked Shreyas very much.

"Aunty, Pranab wants his watch and a water bottle. He is feeling thirsty."

Mrs. Deka was a little puzzled. The water bottle was fine, but why did he need the watch? In two minds, she went to the balcony and held up the water bottle and the watch and called out to Pranab.

Pranab had a clear view of the bottle, but not the watch – or in the heat of the game did not pay much attention. He shouted back – "Yes Mummy, please give it to Shreyas."

The little kid collected the two items and came down to the play area. He called Pranab out and showed the two items. Surprised, Pranab came to the sideline, took the watch and kept staring at Shreyas in total puzzlement. He looked up to their apartment balcony and found his mother standing there waving to him smilingly.

Seeing Pranab with the watch in his hand, the other boys came near and burst out laughing. They had all been involved in the conspiracy and the mystery was no longer one.

The 'Mystery of the Lost Watch' was solved.

The Unraveling

Tejas and Shreyas came back excitedly to their apartment after the game was over. They were all smiles and bursting with excitement to unravel the mystery to their parents and *Ajji*. *Baba* and *Mamma* were having tea after coming home from office.

"*Mamma*, we found the watch!"

The parents smilingly exchanged glances. *Baba* showed surprise – "Where was it?"

"It was in Pranab's house – it was not stolen at all!"

Baba asked - "But how did it all happen?"

Tejas spoke in a torrent of words – "My friends got together and played the prank on me for my birthday party. Arnab was not having fever that day, but stayed back to fool us later. Both the twins attended the Party – one in the morning and the other later."

"Slowly, Tejas! Tell me how did they remove the watch from the house?"

Tejas slowed down to explain properly – "Pranab came in the morning wearing the watch and he removed it and kept it on the shelf as we all went downstairs for playing French Cricket. When we had a break in the game downstairs, he ran out to go to the washroom in the basement. But he did not go to the washroom there and neither did he come back to the game."

"So, who took the watch and when?" *Mamma's* question.

Now Shreyas interjected – "Arnab had come in the meantime and was waiting in the basement. They switched the specs from Pranab to Arnab; then Arnab came back to join us and Pranab came up to our house to take the watch and go back to their apartment."

Ajji said – "Oh, that's the time Pranab came to visit the washroom!"

Mamma asked – "But surely Pranab-Arnab's parents would have detected the switch?"

Tejas said – "It seems that day his parents had gone out for shopping and only their old grandmother was at home. Her eyesight isn't very good."

Baba started laughing – "Now I can tell you kids. In the evening that day I came to know about this prank because Pranab rang me up and told me not to worry. He also told me that it was a prank they had planned for Tejas's birthday celebrations. But I did not know how they had done it. He told me that they would reveal the mystery to you after a few days and till then he requested me to keep silent. But it's remarkable that you boys could unravel the mystery on the third day itself! How did you find out?"

Shreyas said with a serious face – "*Baba*, don't forget we are the 'Little Sherlocks'! We solved the mystery through our observations and information, and of course, our consultant helped us too."

Baba was genuinely surprised this time – "Consultant! What do you mean? Who is he?"

Mamma smilingly said – "Shreyas's dear Mohinder Uncle!"

The whole family burst out laughing.

9. At the farmhouse

An Exciting Proposition

The Joshis were no longer staying in their old establishment at Nagarjuna complex in East Bengaluru. Though they just loved the place because of its cleanliness and every facility nearby, they had been feeling the need for a bigger residence since the boys, the eleven-year-old Tejas and his younger brother Shreyas at eight-and-a-half, were growing up very fast. For proper development of their mental faculties, it was necessary to give them independent space, which was not possible in the Nagarjuna apartment. So, they shifted to the Zucchini Dreamland which was nearer to their workplace, but some conveniences of HSR had to be compromised. They had shifted there about a year ago.

All friends and acquaintances were amused to hear about this peculiar name for this residential complex, and invariably, this would be a topic of amused discussion for first-time guests. The reason given was also unusual, but perhaps logical. The Complex having about 250 villas was built on a 35-acre plot, which was a longish-shaped piece of land and was very green because of a large number of trees the promoters decided not to cut down when the construction started. The result was that the Complex looked like a giant zucchini viewed from the top. For better effect or not, the Promoters decided on this unconventional name for this upscale residential complex for the catchy effect (there was actually an incident which led to this name, the originally intended name was Zumani, but the Promoter's three-year-old grandson pronounced it as Zucchini– the grandfather instantly liked this name and went ahead despite his associates making fun of it).

Tejas and Shreyas were very sorry to leave Nagarjuna where they had grown up since their birth and had a lot of friends. But their parents convinced them about the long-term benefits, and they agreed reluctantly. Of course, since the boys would be going to the same VIRGO school, their friends who studied in the same school would still remain in contact. On the positive side, they would make new friends in Zucchini.

The school summer vacation was not very far off, and often the parents and the kids would discuss the various possibilities about how to spend the days. After all, how many hours could they spend in a day reading books or drawing? Outdoor games during the daytime were out of question in view of the intense heat.

One of the Joshi kids' best friends in the new place was Wasim. He belonged to one of the richest families in Zucchini and was a very pleasant and friendly kid. His father Ahmed was based in Dubai, running a string of businesses and spent almost nine months of the year there. But he made it a point to visit Bengaluru for about a month and a half during the summer – one to avoid the scorching heat in Dubai, and secondly to spend more time with his son and daughter who were in Bengaluru with their mother pursuing their studies.

"Tejas, what is your plan for the summer vacation this year?" asked Wasim while playing football in the complex play area one day.

Tejas seemed uncertain – "I don't know. My parents are working out something, but it may not be much different from what we had been doing during our earlier vacations. It gets very boring actually."

"Want to do something different this time?" There was a quizzical expression on Wasim's face.

"Don't mind at all." Tejas said and looked expectantly at his friend.

Another kid, Akash, urged Wasim – "You seem to have something in mind! Why don't you tell us?"

At the hint of something interesting (to all, since all the kids were faced with a similar situation during this time), the other friends Chetan, Sarvesh, Ian, Venkat and Salim also joined in the exchange – "Come on, Wasim! Share with us too. It would be great if we could all do it together!"

Wasim was pleased to see the response from his friends. He took his time and started explaining – "My father has a very big farmhouse outside Bengaluru. It is really huge and has lots of trees and open areas where we can play. We have been there a few times during summer and found it to be much cooler and more pleasant than here. My parents have suggested that we kids could go to that place and spend a couple of weeks."

"Where is it and how do you reach there?" Sarvesh asked.

"Oh, it is at a place called Shimshapura, about 120 kilometres from Bengaluru. We would have to go by car. There is no other public transport to get there."

Ian had a question – "But how big is it, how many can it accommodate?"

"It is really big with a big building to accommodate all of us. Why don't you all come? We can have a real fun-time there for two weeks."

There were expressions of excitement on the faces of all the kids. It would be different and fun of a different kind!

"We would love to go, Wasim! But we have to seek permission from our parents." Venkat said.

Wasim was happy to note the initial enthusiasm among his friends – "Okay, you all ask your parents and let me know tomorrow. In the meantime, I shall talk to my father so that he can also discuss about the trip with your parents regarding arrangements. Is that okay with you all?"

All the boys nodded happily; only one more hurdle, and then they could have an enjoyable couple of weeks away from the boring environment of Bengaluru during the summer vacation.

Detailed programme

Fortunately for the boys, all the parents were in agreement about the trip, but they wanted to seek clarifications on certain aspects. In anticipation, Ahmed called all the parents in his house on a Sunday morning, two days after Wasim had broached the subject. He knew that the parents would like to be assured of the safety and well-being of their wards during these two weeks of them being out of their eyes' vigil.

After some light savouries and *nimbu-pani* were served to the assembled parents in his house, Ahmed started with an account of the details regarding his farmhouse – "The farmhouse is located at Shimshapura, about 120 kilometres from here. It is located about eight kilometres off the State Highway. The farmhouse is located over an area of 20 acres and is totally walled on all sides with tight security arrangement round the clock. The place has a big building in the centre which can easily and comfortably accommodate all the kids. There is electricity supply from the State grid, and also provision for emergency diesel generator. I have also installed solar water heater and photo-voltaic panels. Groundwater is plenty and I have got it tested for potability. It is perhaps better than what we get in Bengaluru from the Water Supply Department. We have a large area where we grow most of the vegetables for daily consumption and there are plenty of fruit trees like mangoes, guavas, *sapotas*, jackfruits etc. There are about fifty coconut trees in the farm from where we get plenty of coconuts and water all the year round. There is a large pond where fishes are grown. In a nutshell, right inside the farm we get all the natural fruits and vegetables grown only with organic fertilizer. We also have ten cows and buffaloes for all our dairy needs. Once a week, the caretaker and the Estate Manager make a trip to the nearest town to pick up other essential supplies." Ahmed stopped, giving details about all major points.

One worried father asked – "You mentioned about a pond; but is it safe for the kids? If they are not careful, there could an accident."

"Don't worry; it is quite shallow for most parts, not more than three feet deep. Only in its central zone, it is deeper."

One more question - "Who is going to look after the welfare of the kids? Is your family going to stay there for these two weeks?"

Ahmed said – "Yes and no. I have to come back to Bangalore to mind some important business in the city. I shall escort them there with my wife and daughter. Thereafter, I shall come back alone and go back on the last day to bring them back. My wife will look after their total needs during these two weeks. We also have an excellent Estate Manager to supervise all affairs, and a local couple who stay in the farmhouse itself to meet every aspect of well-being for the visitors. Let me tell you, they are extremely good and caring in their jobs!"

Akash Joshi asked – "How will they spend their time? Are there any recreational facilities in the farmhouse?"

Ahmed answered – "We have a big hall where I have put a table-tennis board and a carrom board. There are plenty of clear open areas where they can play badminton, cricket or football. But these boys will work out all that they could possibly do among themselves, so don't worry about how they spend their time."

"What about medical attention, in case it is necessary?" Justin's father asked.

"The Estate Manager keeps a supply of common medical supplies for emergencies and knows a little bit about what to do immediately. But we rush the sick immediately to the nearby town hospital if the problem is beyond his capabilities."

Most of the relevant issues were raised and clarified. In the end, the parents were satisfied that their boys would be safe and happy in the farmhouse for the two weeks of their stay. Only one question remained and hesitantly someone asked – "What is the arrangement for transport?" Shimshapura was too far for the parents to drive their kids individually.

"Don't bother at all! I shall arrange a large SUV in addition to my own car. These two vehicles should be able to accommodate all the children comfortably."

Wasim's friend Justin from VIRGO School also had indicated his willingness. That made it twelve boys in all. 'The Dirty Dozen' – Ahmed had jokingly nick-named this group of twelve.

Arrival and Problem

The following Sunday was the day of departure for the sojourn at the farmhouse. Ahmed, his family and the dozen kids could all be accommodated in the two large SUVs. The parents came to see their wards off. Every family had prepared some dry snacks for all the kids to munch and enjoy during their stay at the farmhouse and loaded the goodies in the vehicles. The kids were all in high spirits.

Collectively they had organized to carry cricket kits, badminton racquets, table-tennis bats, football and some board games such as Scrabble, Monopoly etc., to keep themselves occupied. Tejas, the avid reader, was carrying an old Kindle, which his Mamma had, but was not using.

They reached the place after a journey of about two-and-a-half hours. They had started early to avoid the heat and the traffic – and it was a good decision. The kids started a cacophony in the vehicles during the early part of the journey; but dozed off during the latter part.

The farmhouse was rightly named 'The Oasis', because it was an island of greenery and bountiful natural elements in the midst of arid and barren surroundings. It was evident that the staff had worked very hard to create and maintain this pleasant and comfortable place out of nowhere.

Wasim's mother Sufiya immediately made arrangements for refreshments and meals for the young boys. She also introduced the Estate Manager (EM) Srinivas and the caretaker couple Rudrappa and Shanthamma to the boys; clear instructions were given to the staff to take utmost care for the young guests. On arrival, the boys were given fresh coconut water from the farmhouse trees.

The twelve boys were accommodated in three big rooms on the first floor. There were many comfortable mattresses in the building. One of the boys asked Wasim – "Your Dad has arranged for so many beds for us?"

The Host boy smiled and replied – "Let me tell you a secret – my Abbu intends to convert this farmhouse to a resort for the tourists. Let me show you the cottages being constructed around the place." He took them to the balcony around the rooms and showed the construction in progress a little distance away. "These bed materials have been purchased in advance." He added.

The boys had a simple food of egg curry and rice for lunch. Venkat was the only vegetarian, and a vegetable curry was prepared for him. There was curd for everyone.

At around five O'clock, all the boys came down and went to the open area in front of the building to play football. Beyond the open ground were thick bushes and shrubs and beyond that the compound wall. About half a dozen coconut trees were arranged in a line along the wall. A little bit to the side was the mango orchard. About a dozen mango trees were grown there, and this time of year being the mango season, the trees were full of ripe and luscious mangoes. It was indeed a sight to behold and admire! While playing football, the gaze of the boys often fell on these trees and they looked forward to partaking the delicious mangoes during their stay.

During the game of football, the ball fell into the bushes a number of times and one of the boys would go and retrieve from the thicket of bushes and shrubs. On one occasion, it fell into a particularly dense area and Chetan ran into the thicket to retrieve the ball.

He did it, but not without some damage to himself. He came back scratching his arms, legs and his face irritably slowly at first, but as moments passed by, he started scratching more vigorously with increasing discomfort. Very soon the irritation was so much that, though he was a big boy, he started howling and crying and started rolling on the ground. Hearing all the commotion, Sufiya came running to the area followed by Srinivas. The EM enquired with the boys about what led to the present situation and quickly went inside and came out with some tube of ointment. This he applied on Chetan's body, which by now had large angry red blotches in the areas that were exposed and had come into contact with the bushes.

The poor boy forgot about the game and sat by the side still in terrible discomfort.

The EM said – "Boys, let me point out these dangerous plants to you. These are called 'Stinging Nettles'. Never let the leaves of these plants come in contact with any exposed part of your skin. Even if your football falls in those bushes, use a stick to retrieve and never walk into them. You have seen what a terrible problem these plants can cause." He took the boys and showed them the plants and the spots where they grew.

"Why don't you cut and remove them, Uncle?" Asked Ian.

Srinivas gravely shook his head – "We do; but these plants grow so fast that within no time at all, they grow back to their full size. It's almost a losing game for us."

Chetan was back in his elements only by the next morning. He had spent a disturbed night due to the discomfort of the rashes on his body.

Mango Thieves

At breakfast the next morning, the boys expected an abundance of ripe mangoes, but there were only a few. Some of them expressed their surprise to Wasim who approached the EM. Srinivas walked over to the table where the boys were sitting for their breakfast. He looked a little embarrassed.

"There is a small problem with the mangoes this year - the mangoes are being stolen."

"How, Uncle?" Venkat asked.

"Well, you see there is a group of huts just beyond the farmhouse compound where the construction workers are staying. I suspect that some of the young boys from those huts are stealing the mangoes."

"But if you know that, why are you not catching them?" asked Sarvesh.

"Unless we catch them red-handed, how can we level charges at them? We did accuse them on a couple of occasions, but they denied their involvement outright."

"But the compound has security gate and high walls. How are they entering?" Tejas's question.

Srinivas made a gesture for them to come out of the dining room, and from the edge of the building pointed out to a portion of the compound wall – "Do you see those two coconut trees very close to the wall? Those are almost touching the wall. I have a feeling that the thieves are climbing up to the wall on the other side by some means and then climbing down into the compound by clinging to the trunk of those coconut trees. Their huts are also very close to the other side of the wall."

"Can your guards not catch them when they climb down?" Shreyas asked.

"I think they are doing it very late in the night when the guards also doze off, and they do it so silently, that there is no sound."

The boys came back into the dining room and silently ate their breakfast. Justin saw Tejas and Shreyas talking in a low voice. He had come to know that the Joshi brothers had earlier solved some puzzling problems in their previous place of stay – Nagarjuna. He said – "Come on Tejas, you think you can come up with a solution?"

Tejas did not answer but continued to think seriously.

Shreyas was a sympathetic kid. He kept looking at Chetan who still had the remnants of the red blotches on his body and still felt itchy to some extent.

"Chetan, how are you feeling now?" Shreyas asked.

"Better, but I would never go anywhere near those nettle plants in my lifetime again."

Shreyas kept looking at the suffering boy absent-mindedly, but clearly his mind was active elsewhere.

After a few minutes, there was a faint smile on his face and he got up.

"I have an idea how those mango thieves can be taught a lesson. Come to the ground and I shall tell you." The boys were surprised that the youngest among them had come up with a solution, but having heard of the exploits of the Joshi brothers, they followed curiously.

There were discussions among them and a few short sorties to the compound wall and to the spots where the mango and coconut trees were standing. In the end, they were amused with the solution and wanted to give it a try.

Shreyas then addressed Wasim – "Wasim, we require the following items in the afternoon –

1. A couple of sharp choppers

2. Some lengths of thick strings

3. Three or four leather or rubber hand gloves

4. A few caps

5. Some thin towels or cloth.

Wasim said it was not a problem – gloves were available because the cows and buffaloes were milked with the gloves on, and the other items were no problem at all.

At about four O'clock, the boys descended on the ground and walked to the edge of the bushes on the other side. By agreement, they had all come in full trousers, full-sleeve shirts and shoes. Now they put the caps on their heads, wrapped the thin towels on their faces leaving only the eyes open, put the gloves on their hands and started chopping down the 'Stinging Nettle' plants.

Before sunset, they had finished their work and were satisfied that the mango thieves would be taught a lesson.

The boys formed two batches of six each and decided to keep watch from the ground floor balcony by taking turns. One batch would watch while the other slept, and after three hours they would switch the watch. The wakeful batch also would keep the night batch of security guards on their toes.

The first shift started at ten at night.

Now, it was only another case of 'Watch and Catch'.

Nothing happened during the first shift. The second batch took over at one O'clock after midnight. The area where the mango trees were located, was pitch dark and nothing could be seen. The boys kept sitting in the dark balcony braving the irritating mosquitoes.

After about an hour, there were cries of pain and anguish from the mango trees area. The boys heard that and blew a whistle (borrowed from the guards earlier). Hearing the sound in the stillness of the night, the guards ran quickly in that direction. The other boys who had gone to rest were also awakened and joined the apprehenders. There were two powerful torchlights with them.

There were four young men in their mid-teens who were obviously in trouble, scratching their bodies with anguished grimaces on their faces. The young men were apprehended by the security guards and another batch went around to the other side of the wall and caught two others who were waiting to receive the loot. Their modus operandi was that the young men inside would climb the mango trees, pluck the fruits, pack them in polythene bags and hoist the bags over the wall with the help of a long rope. The process would repeat a few times before they would escape in a similar way after collecting ample loot.

Wasim and his mates had wrapped some of the cut branches of the Nettle plants around the coconut and mango trees' trunks and dumped the rest near the bases. The intruders had no idea of the lurking danger and rubbed against them while climbing down the coconut trees and climbing up the mango trees to pluck the fruits. Then the extreme itching and discomfort started a few moments later.

The security guards kept the intruders locked up in a room for the rest of the night and brought them in front of Ahmed (who was to leave for Bengaluru a little later in the morning). The young men were from the families of the construction workers who were called and served severe warning. The guilty were allowed to go only after their parents vowed to take their wards to task so that the acts were not repeated in future.

The owner of the farmhouse was impressed by the planning and teamwork of the young boys and congratulated them.

During the subsequent days, there was no dearth of ripe delicious mangoes on the table.

The Fishing Trip

The rest of the stay for the boys at 'The Oasis' was full of enjoyment and fun. They would wake up early in the morning (without anybody pushing them) and go for a walk around the farmhouse and beyond without going too far. The very sight of various plants, trees and birds they had never seen before in the city was energizing for their minds. The food made with farm-fresh products on the table was truly delicious. They played both indoor and outdoor games, and the kits they had brought along proved handy.

One day, Srinivas told them – "There is a creek about half a kilometer away from the farmhouse. Would you boys like to go for fishing one day?"

The boys were overjoyed. Being city-bred boys, they had never got such opportunities before. All of them raised their hands with cheers.

"Okay then, we can go tomorrow early morning or just before evening. These times are most suited for fishing."

Wasim said that during his earlier trips to the farmhouse, he and his sister also had gone for fishing in the same creek - "It would be such fun." – He said. But there was the hint of a smile on his face.

Tejas said – "I remember we had gone to an estate a few years back and gone for a similar fishing activity. Both of us were very young at that time. Let us see this time."

Shreyas had a doubt – "But Uncle, how do we catch fish? Do we use a net?"

Tejas affectionately ruffled the hair on his younger brother's head – "Oh my naïve brother! You use a fishing rod in small places. Nets are used in big lakes and rivers. But Uncle, do you have the fishing rods?"

Wasim said – "Yes, we have. Srinivas uncle keeps four fishing rods for us. Even my Ammi tried her hand sometimes."

They went for fishing in the late afternoon next day. Four fishing rods and a big lump of dough made with wheat flour were taken along. The boys left with a feeling of adventure. Srinivas also came with them.

They walked over the rough terrain outside for about half a kilometer before they came to the creek. It was not wide but had flowing water. Srinivas pointed out one spot where the creek was wide and a portion of stationery water could be seen.

"That's the spot where you can try to catch the fish." The boys could see plenty of small sized fish swimming around in the water at that spot.

Soon the boys took turns with the fishing rods. A small ball of dough was stuck at the tip of the hook as the bait and the line was lowered into the water. A small piece of plastic tied to the line remained floating above the surface of the water. Any jerky movement of the plastic would indicate nibbling of the bait by the fish. That was the time the angler (one who was trying to catch the fish) was supposed to give a sudden pull with the rod to stick the hook in the mouth of the fish. But in reality, every time, the fish managed to eat the bait and get away without getting stuck in the hook. Wasim kept smiling as he watched his friends struggle with the rods.

It was nearing sunset and the light was fading, and they had to trek the half kilometer back to the farmhouse. Srinivas instructed the boys to wrap up the adventure for the day and return.

"It is difficult to catch these fish. They are too crafty." – said Srinivas on the way.

Now Wasim had a laugh – "Now I can tell you mates, we also could never catch a single fish. They are cleverer than us. I didn't want to kill your excitement by warning in advance."

Chetan said enthusiastically – "That's alright Wasim! Even with no catch, we had an enjoyable outing." It was good to see him come out of the trauma of the 'Stinging Nettles'.

The sky was getting darker by the minute and they realized that it was not all due to the setting sun – there were dark clouds overhead. Halfway to the safety of the farmhouse, it started raining heavily. Since the sky was bright and clear when they had set out for the fishing trip, nobody had thought about carrying an umbrella. With no place nearby to take shelter, they had no option but to walk through the rain. 'If you can't avoid it, enjoy it' –and so the boys kept cheering one another and enjoyed getting drenched in the rain to make light of their troubles.

Fortunately, none of them caught fever or any other type of problem despite the exposure.

Picnic and Loss

Before they realized, they were on the penultimate day of their stay at the farmhouse – the two-week period had passed quickly and enjoyably. Ahmed would come in the evening with the second SUV to escort the boys back to the city. The boys had enjoyed the outing very much and wanted to conclude the outing with something new.

"Can we organize a table-tennis competition today?" – asked Ian.

"What's new about it? We can always do that back in the city also." – quipped Sarvesh.

"Perhaps a hide and seek game in the compound?" – Justin's suggestion.

Wasim was quiet and was thinking. He suddenly got an idea – "Those are old hats, boys. I have an idea – something you have not done before – a picnic in the wild!"

"Wild? Where is the wild here?" – Tejas asked.

"Not that kind of wild, man! We can have a picnic in the midst of some jungle-like area in our compound itself. There are places where you feel you are inside a mini forest."

The idea generally appealed to all. It remained only to choose a spot.

Akash took it another step further – "It will be fun if we cook ourselves."

Now it was getting really interesting! There was vociferous support for both the suggestions.

Shreyas put a dampener – "But who will cook?"

The boys had not given a serious thought to this question. They kept glancing at one another.

Shreyas said – "*Dada* keeps writing about recipes in his book. Perhaps he can help."

Justin was the oldest boy in the group. and said – "Don't worry! We can all put our hands together and cook. It doesn't matter if the food is not as good as Shanthamma aunty's."

The Estate Manager Srinivas was passing by; seeing the boys in animated discussion, he stopped and asked jokingly – "What's cooking, boys?"

Shreyas was the one with the quickest wit; he said – "Not yet cooking, Uncle, but we really want to cook."

Srinivas was amused – "You want to cook! Whatever for?"

Wasim came up – "Uncle, it is our last day today and we want to do something different and new. We were planning to have a picnic in the forest area inside. Can you suggest a spot?"

Srinivas was also a sportive person. He liked the idea and said – "Come with me, I shall show you a nice spot."

They all went together to the spot with Srinivas. It was a wooded area by the side of the pond. There was a clear space surrounded by tall trees and bamboo thickets. It was cool, comfortable and very convenient.

Srinivas said – "Last year some friends of Ahmed Sir came to spend a few days here and they organized a picnic at this spot."

The boys were very happy and decided to have the picnic at that very spot.

As they were going back to the main building, Srinivas asked – "But what about your food?"

"We shall cook ourselves, Uncle. That would be a lot of fun" – Wasim said.

Srinivas stopped in his tracks and shook his head slightly – "You better check with your mother on that issue, Wasim."

Wasim's mother Sufiya's reaction to the boys' plan was mixed. She liked the idea of having a picnic in the forest area, but totally ruled out the plan for their cooking the food.

"No chance, boys! I don't want you to take any risk with the fire and hot oil for the cooking. Rudrappa and Shanthamma will do the cooking there but you people can help them with cutting and cleaning. That would be a nice experience without the risks." Then she added a sweetener – "Asma and I also would join your picnic." Asma was Wasim's elder sister.

The boys accepted this solution. It would still be great fun.

The picnic was a great success. The food was simple but delicious – *khichdi*, some *bhajjis*, vegetable curry and egg curry plus *gulab jamuns* at the end. The pool added to the beauty of the place. There was still clear water in the pool and fishes could be seen swimming in the deep. After their futile fishing experience at the creek, some of them tried the fishing rods at the pool. The result was no better.

The boys ran around, played *kabaddi* in the clear area and tried playing *antakshari* with Asma taking the role of the anchor. When they were going back to the main building in the late afternoon, they were thrilled with the new experience. Where in the city would they get the chance for a picnic in the wild? A fitting finale to their summer outing!

Ahmed had arrived by then and all of them were to start back for Bengaluru after breakfast next morning.

And then the spell of 'feeling good' was shattered!

Boys on the Job

Salim exclaimed as they were all entering the building – "Oh no! Where is my ring?"

Salim had come for the trip with a gold ring on his finger. It was an attractive ring with a green emerald-like stone set in the middle. The ring had caught the attention of the other boys also and when they had enquired, Salim had said that recently his grandmother had gifted it to him on his 11th birthday.

"But why did you come to this trip with such a costly ring, Salim?" – Someone asked.

"I usually like to wear it. I had intended to take it off before coming, but forgot at the end because of the hurry. Now, my *Ammi* will take me to task seriously!"

"When did you see it last on your finger?" Venkat asked.

"I remember fiddling with it when I was cutting some vegetables, but between then and now, I don't know when I lost it."

Tejas with his logical mind tried to calm down the distraught boy – "Salim, now calm down and think coolly what all you did after cutting the vegetables?"

Salim closed his eyes and tried to think of his activities in sequence – "I wanted to see how Shanthamma Aunty prepared the food. So, while you all were busy playing games, I was in the cooking area only."

"Then?"

"We all sat down for food after that. Nothing much happened after that. Oh, I remember now – I had the ring at that time. I changed it from left hand to right hand for eating." Salim was a left-hander.

Justin said – "After food, we played *antakshari* and then came back here. So, it must have been lost during this period."

Tejas said – "Let us go back to the picnic area and search. We shall all keep watching the path we took to come back here. It should still be on the ground if it fell from the finger while walking. Salim, was the ring a little loose on your finger?"

Salim said – "Not on my left-hand finger; but a little loose on my right."

The boys retraced their path to the picnic spot very slowly and kept looking on both sides. But they could not see anything like a metal ring.

Next the cooking area was searched thoroughly. All the cooking implements had been placed on a *durree* spread on the ground, and it was still there. Thorough search was carried out – but unsuccessfully.

The only place remained was the place where the boys had sat on the ground and played *antakshari*. It must be there, then!

A vigorous search yielded nothing there also. Now the boys were in low spirits and thinking about what to do next when Shreyas quietly asked Salim – "Where did you wash your hands after food, Salim?"

The boy said – "In the pool over there; do you see the paved area with a few steps? I did not go down all the steps but just reached where the water came up to the steps."

Shreyas quietly went there and sat down on the lowest dry step and looked intently at the water nearby. He kept looking very patiently.

The boys gave up their search and started walking back dejectedly. Shreyas was still sitting on the step by the water. Nobody noticed him.

As the boys came back and sat down in the hall in a sad mood, Shreyas came in running.

"Salim, here is your ring!"

As a much relieved and surprised Salim kept looking at his dear ring, the others were no less surprised.

"Where did you find it, Shreyas?" Tejas asked.

Shreyas calmly said – "It was in the water of the pool."

"But how did you know that it was there?"

"When you think logically, you cover every step. All of you searched all the areas Salim had been to except one – that was at the pool to wash his hands. I went there and searched under the water surface. The glittering gold was clearly visible." He coolly picked up a piece of cake from the dining table.

"Fortunately, the pool water was very clear" – he added.

10. Crafty Pilferer

Summer Camp Announcement

There was an announcement during the assembly at the VIRGO School (Bengaluru) one March morning; it was a few days before the summer vacation was to begin.

The Principal was speaking – "Children, we are happy to tell you that this year the Management of Junior Boys' Scout have decided to hold a Summer Camp for fifteen days starting 10th of April. Those of you, who are enrolled with them as Scouts, would automatically be eligible to join the Camp. If the needed numbers of volunteers are not available, then the others, who are not members of the Junior Scouts, may be considered, but their participation is not guaranteed. You will find the details on the main notice board. This will be an opportunity for the volunteers to spend good time in learning things that you don't get to know in normal classroom teachings. My advice is that such an opportunity should not be wasted. You can see the notice board and if you find the programme interesting, you can collect a copy of the details from the school office for discussing with your parents."

Tejas had grown up to be twelve years old and would be going to the seventh standard after the summer vacation. He was a very alert and intelligent kid who liked to keep an eye on all happenings around him and tried to find logical answers to all issues in life. He had already enrolled for the Junior Boys' Scouts about six months earlier on his *Mamma's* urging (she was also a *'Bulbul'* for the Girls' Scouts during her student days in Hyderabad), and therefore, quite thrilled to be presented with this Camp opportunity.

There was no time to see the notice board before going to their classroom for the lessons and therefore, Tejas waited for the lunch break and after finishing his lunch quickly in the School Canteen went to see the notice board. In the meantime, he had discussed the matter with his friends Apurv, Justin and Madhava – who were also enrolled as Scouts. The four friends quickly read the contents of the announcement and found the programme to their liking.

"I am all for it! What about you?" – Tejas announced.

"Yes" said Madhava.

"Me too" was Justin's reply.

The three now looked at Apurv, the boy was hesitating – "I don't know! I have never stayed outside my home for fifteen days. So, I am a little scared" – there was an uneasy smile on his face. Apurv was the only child of his parents and was fussed over quite a bit.

Justin was a big boy. He put his hands around Apurv's shoulders – "That's the idea! You get to learn to manage things on your own. After all, you cannot stay with your parents all your life. Why do you worry? We are all there to help one another."

Apurv let go of his unease – "Okay then, I am also in."

Tejas said – "But guys, we still have to get permission from our parents. If they agree, we shall have a great time."

They quickly walked over to the School Office and collected the announcement paper copies.

The Approval

That evening Tejas waited for his parents to relax for some time over a cup of tea after they came back from their office. He knew that it would be wrong to hustle them immediately after setting foot in the house after a long and tiring drive through the busy evening traffic of Bengaluru.

"*Baba*, take a look at this announcement. There is going to be a Summer Camp for the Junior Boys' Scouts next month. It seems to be very interesting. If you and *Mamma* agree, I would like to attend."

This was a problem area for most of the parents in a city (if both were working professionals) during the summer vacation. Every year around this time, *Baba* and *Mamma* would be out of their wits to find ways to keep the two hyperactive kids (Tejas and his younger brother Shreyas who was nine-and-a-half) busy during the daytime. In fact, while returning from the office, they were discussing this matter. Usually they used to send the kids to *Advaitham* or Global Art (both small establishments keeping the children occupied with painting, crafts and other small engagements) during the daytime. The kids were bored with the same type of activities every year and wanted to do something different this time.

Now this Camp opportunity spared the parents the effort of looking for alternatives; and it wasn't a bad idea at all!

As *Baba* finished going through the paper, *Mamma* asked – "Akash, can you please tell me about it?"

Baba handed over the paper to *Mamma* and said – "You can go through it later; but let me tell you the gist of it.

The Camp is for fifteen days. It starts on 10th April and ends on 24th. It is going to be held in an interior village area 20 kilometres from Dodballapur (Dodballapur was a satellite town of the Bengaluru city roughly 50 kilometres away). The fees are Rupees five thousand per volunteer. During the Camp, the children would learn story-telling, theme building, nature walk, observation and report writing, debating and presentation sessions, basics of gardening etc. in addition to sports activities. But in my opinion, there are two more important things they would go through; one is, daily physical exercise in the early morning, and secondly, learning how to manage all personal necessities on their own including washing their own clothes and making their own beds. It is high time they start becoming self-sufficient."

Mamma said – "Wow! We send a child to the Camp, and he comes back as a grown-up! But will they be staying in an open campsite? Will it be very hot out there?"

"No, it seems there is a residential convent school and the premises are available during the summer vacation as all the inmates go home. It is also surrounded by a forest and remains much cooler than the city. I think it is a wonderful opportunity; what do you feel?"

Mamma thought for a while and nodded – "I agree with you, and the charges are reasonable also. These small establishments here charge two thousand Rupees just to keep the kid busy for two hours per day without giving any refreshments at all for only fifteen days. Let's do it. Tejas, are you keen on this Camp?"

Tejas was all this while following his parents' conversation and he said – "Yes, *Mamma*. Not only me; my friends Apurv, Justin and Madhava also have said they would come. I think more friends would agree to join us tomorrow. It would be fun with all of us together."

Baba and *Mamma* exchanged glances and smiled – so these kids had already worked out plans of their own! *Mamma* said – "We don't know anything about the organizers; will it not be risky to send young boys without enquiring?"

Tejas very innocently played his card – "If you do not agree, I won't insist on going."

Baba said – "Don't worry Tejas, we are agreeable; but we shall also enquire in the school about the organizers before giving our final decision."

Shreyas was lurking nearby; he now came forward – "What about me, *Mamma*? I also want to go to the Camp with *Dada*."

Baba said – "That would have been wonderful Shreyas, but you have to be at least twelve years old if you are to be considered."

Shreyas understood; he was still not old enough. He said – "Then without *Dada* in the house, what shall I do alone?"

Mamma smilingly said – "We shall work out something interesting for you here; or we may send you to Hyderabad to spend some time with *Dadu* and *Nimma*. You can solve some problem there like you did during your last visit." She then turned to Akash and said – "Let's talk to the Principal tomorrow."

Aditi rang up the principal of VIRGO School next morning at ten. When she mentioned about the Camp, the Principal said – "There are many like you who have rung me up on this. To answer all your questions, I have invited the Coordinator of this Camp on

Saturday, at eleven O'clock. Please come and attend for clarifications."

Tejas's friend and classmate Justin was full of excitement in the morning when the boys met just before the assembly – "Mates, my parents have agreed for the trip; and you know what – the person who is organizing the trip is my uncle, my mother's first cousin! His name is Milind Cyrus. I've known him since I was a baby and he is a very nice person."

Apurv asked – "Is he also going to be there with us in the Camp?"

"Yes, he told my mother it is going to be great fun and we shouldn't miss it."

The others said in unison – "Then we are all going, unless our parents seriously object."

Clarifications

As communicated by the Principal earlier, the parents of the interested students were there in the school on Saturday morning. There were many and the hall was full. Before the Camp Coordinator arrived, there was a buzz in the hall – curious parents started checking with one another about various issues on their minds.

Precisely at eleven, the Principal entered the hall accompanied by the Camp Coordinator, Mr. Milind Cyrus. He seemed to be around forty years of age, tall and athletic and possessed a pleasant expression on his face. He cheerily waved to all the waiting parents.

The Principal opened the conversation – "Good morning. You certainly have a lot of questions on your minds and so I won't take much time. Meet Mr. Milind Cyrus – he is an ex-volleyball player who had represented the State in the Nationals and has been organizing this kind of Camp for the last five years. If I am not mistaken, this is his 21st Camp; am I right, Mr. Cyrus?" She turned and looked at the guest. The Coordinator nodded smilingly.

The Principal continued - "I have made enquiries to ascertain that the earlier Camps were professionally conducted and there were no complaints from parents; only then I permitted our School's involvement. Now ladies and gentlemen, it's over to Mr. Cyrus."

Milind Cyrus strode forward, wished everybody a Good Morning and briefly gave an outline of the Camp; then he invited queries from the assembled.

One father raised his hand – "What kind of security would be there for the boys? I understand it is right in the middle of a forest area?" A valid point, since kidnapping for ransom these days was becoming a lucrative business for the underworld criminals.

Cyrus smiled – "Good point! I am glad that this question came up first. Let me answer you to put your fears to rest. The Holy Angels' Residential School, including the living quarters of the students, is surrounded by ten feet walls. A professional security team is in charge of the only entrance gate and there is patrolling both inside and the outside of the walls round the clock. Without legitimate passes with ID, no outsider is allowed to enter the campus." He paused for a few moments and then added for effect – "You may be surprised to know that I myself had studied in this residential school up to my high school and during my stay for eight years there, there was not a single instance of security breach."

This revelation brought murmurs, whispers and exclamations from those present; Cyrus's last sentence effectively settled all security concerns.

Another mother from the front row stood up and asked – "Can you tell us what kind of food will be given to the boys? Will there only be vegetarian food?".

"We shall arrange for eggs to be given every day during breakfast and chicken dish additionally during dinner. But even the vegetarian dishes would be wholesome and nutritious. We also pay very close attention to hygiene aspects." The mother sat down satisfied.

Akash asked – "What is the arrangement for medical emergencies?"

Cyrus raised his index finger and appreciated the question by nodding his head with a smile – "Thank you for bringing this up; I was definitely going to raise this point myself. Nothing is more important than ensuring the well-being of the young kids so far away from the city. We are being accompanied by a General Physician from the city and he would stay with us in the campus for the entire fifteen days. In addition, we have linked up with the best private hospital at Dodballapur for any other emergencies round the clock."

Akash seemed to be satisfied with the answer.

The Q & A session went on for some time and at the end, all those present had their queries effectively answered. Cyrus finally summed up the salient points of the Camp

1. A total of 250 boys could be accommodated in the Camp.

2.   A medium size suitcase should accommodate all essentials of the volunteer.

3.   No cash should be kept with the boys; also, no expensive electronic gadgets.

4.   The School Library has a rich collection of books to read; no need to carry additional books.

5.   Sports shoes should be carried for the games. A compact folding umbrella would be handy in case of rain.

6.   If the volunteer is under a regular medication, then sufficient stock should be packed in his bag.

Most of the essential instructions were communicated during this interaction. Before departure, Cyrus said – "My only request is – please make up your mind fast, as we can accommodate only 250 in all and many schools are interested."

The Journey

A total of 25 students from VIRGO enrolled for the Camp by the cut-off date. Tejas was delighted to know that his best friend Rajesh too was joining them.

On 10th April, Akash dropped Tejas at the spot from where the Camp Bus was to start. Tejas had packed one suitcase and also had a small backpack on his person. Shreyas also came along and wished his elder brother a good time at the Camp. He wished he could also join, but that was not to be!

As the forty boys got into the bus, there were cheers and exclamations of joy from everybody. Since the buses planned to start at seven in the morning to avoid the traffic on the road, the Organizers had arranged for fruits, cakes and fruit juices to be distributed in the bus itself. Packets of biscuits were kept standby in case any of the kids felt hungry during the trip. A proper breakfast was to be served once they reached the Camp, expected journey time being three hours.

Boys Love It

The boys loved the Camp site the moment the buses entered the secured area. There were tall trees all around and the buildings looked well-maintained and clean; there was a big playground in the middle and other indoor games facilities in the Common Room of the hostel. A well-stocked Library was really inviting for avid book readers (like Tejas). The most pleasing aspect was the coolness even at ten O'clock in the morning compared to the heat of the city.

Since the boys were hungry by now, they were immediately sent to the Canteen for a breakfast of *Upma* and *Mysore Bajji,* which could be prepared quickly. No eggs were given on the first day.

After the breakfast, Cyrus (he was accompanied by five other Supervisors, each looking after a specific area) announced that the boys could collect their bags and go to the dormitories on the first floor.

"Choose your beds as per your liking, but don't fight with one another" – he said.

Tejas and his four friends could get five adjacent beds in the dormitory on the first floor. There were clean sheets and a comfortable pillow on each bed. The dorm was well-lit and ventilated. The boys felt happy about the environment and were eager to get into the Camp activities at the earliest.

In the evening, Cyrus and his team addressed all the boys in the open ground (before it became too dark) and outlined the daily schedule of activities starting with physical exercises at six in the morning and ending with dinner at seven thirty in the evening. He emphasized about two things in particular – compliance with the Camp discipline and maintaining brotherly relations with one another in every matter. Nobody was allowed to go outside the main gate unless accompanied by the Camp Coordinator or the Supervisors.

Life went on smoothly and enjoyably for the boys and they made new friends. The food was tasty but not spicy and after the day's activities the boys felt ravenously hungry and ate well. In the late afternoons, they played games of football outside and table tennis and badminton in the indoor area. Cyrus had formed eight teams among the boys for a football tournament over the next two weeks and promised attractive prizes for the winners. The intense but healthy competition generated a lot of interest among the players and non-players alike.

Cyrus kept talking to his nephew Justin from time to time, but showed no preferential treatment to him. That was comfortable with the boy, but he used to feel embarrassed whenever his uncle addressed him as 'Just Baby'; "He always called me that since my childhood" was the shy explanation to his friends. Justin also introduced his four other close friends from his school to his uncle.

Life at the Camp went on smoothly for three days and the boys were very happy that they had chosen to come. They were also learning to take care of their personal necessities like washing their own clothes, making their own beds, keeping their articles organized and tidy, and more. Parents would be extremely happy to notice this development when they were back after the Camp.

And then things started going wrong from the fourth day!

Problems Surface

Fruits were in short supply for breakfast on the fourth morning. Only eighty percent of the boys, who came early, got the apples; the rest didn't.

Some of the older boys approached the Canteen Supervisor and reported the shortage. The Supervisor was genuinely surprised – "How can that be? We always serve all food items adequately for all the participants; in fact, we keep a few extras also." He went to the mess area and enquired, but could not find any answer.

The boys kept quiet; it could always happen and after all what could they do?

Further shocks were in store at dinner time – about fifty boys who came a little late for dinner, found only gravy in chicken curry, but no meat! Again, the Supervisor was approached, but the result was the same – no clue to the reason for shortage.

Both Tejas and Justin were fond of meat and a little annoyed at not getting their favourite dish. They sat down on the bed after dinner and called Rajesh, who being a heathy eater, and perhaps fonder of chicken than the rest, was grumbling at missing his favourite dish.

"Something is fishy! It can't happen two times a day without any explanation from the Supervisors" – said Rajesh.

"Are they serving more to the boys who came early and that's why the late-comers did not get any?" Justin offered a possibility.

Tejas was thinking deeply – "Or could it be that the Canteen people are eating more so that not enough is left for us?"

Apurv and Madhava also joined the discussions as they had also missed apples in the morning.

Apurv said – "No! Nobody is given extra servings any time. It is clearly a case of short supply."

Madhava was the strict vegetarian among them; he jokingly said – "Good, it is better to avoid non-vegetarian food for better health."

Rajesh the avid non-vegetarian said sharply – "Enough Madhava! Let's put our heads together to get to the truth."

"I think somebody is pilfering the valuable items from the Canteen; but who can it be? Outsiders are not allowed into the campus here and Cyrus uncle's people would not do it!" Tejas expressed his view.

Justin said – "It's not that the outside people are not allowed; we have those cleaning ladies and the Canteen helpers."

Rajesh said with some amusement – "Tejas, you have a case on your hand. Remember you and Shreyas had solved a number of theft problems in Nagarjuna?"

Apurv came up promptly – "And that hygiene problem in our School Canteen? We did it as a team with you as the leader!"

Tejas said gravely – "Justin, we have to talk to Cyrus uncle; do you think he will get upset if we go to him now?'

"Not at all! After all, I am his favourite nephew! But not all of us – let you and I go."

So, the two of them went downstairs where Cyrus was staying in a small room. Justin knocked on the door.

"Come in; the door is not locked" – came the voice from inside.

Cyrus was going through the day-to-day expenses of the Camp when the two boys came in. He put the papers down and smiled at the boy who had grown up before his own eyes.

"Ah, Just Baby! What brings you here at this time and with Tejas too?"

Justin's mind was fully on the problem at hand and so he did not think anything about the embarrassing nick-name.

"Uncle, are you aware of the problem in the Canteen?" He asked.

Cyrus was surprised; of all people, these little kids were talking about Canteen problem and that too at this late hour! He said – "Well, when we run a Canteen for 250 children, there are bound to be problems. What are you talking about?"

Tejas intervened – "Uncle, this morning there was a shortage of apples; and many of us did not get any meat in the evening."

There was a frown on Cyrus's forehead. If this was the case, then yes, the boys were talking about a real problem!

"Oh yes, I am aware of it; Kumar told me a little while ago." Kumar was the Canteen Supervisor to whom the shortages had first been pointed out. "There is no reason why there should be any shortage."

"Uncle, is it possible that the cooks and the Canteen helpers are eating it up - more than what they should?" Justin asked again.

"No, my dear! These cooks are all vegetarians and have been working for me for a long time; they wouldn't do such a thing."

"What about the helpers? Did they also come from Bengaluru?"

"No, there is no point in bringing so many non-essential workers from the city. These people are all locals; they work for us on daily wage basis."

Tejas asked – "Apart from these, does anybody else come inside?"

Cyrus said – "Yes, you must have seen those cleaning ladies. But they don't enter the Canteen and go away by mid-day."

"Those who do not stay here – are they allowed taking out stuff while leaving?"

THE LITTLE JASOOS & OTHER STORIES

"No. Anything to be taken out has to be with a written note from the Canteen Supervisor or me; otherwise the security guards would confiscate those items at the gate. But boys, why are you asking me all these questions? Are you two playing Holmes and Watson?" Cyrus laughed at his own wit, even at the moment of being faced with a problem.

But, Tejas was not smiling – "But Uncle, while we were playing football around evening, we have seen some workers leaving with big heavy carry bags in their hands. Who are they and what do they carry in those bags?"

For a moment Cyrus was clueless; then he suddenly remembered – "Oh, those men? They are Canteen helpers from the local areas."

"What do they carry?"

Cyrus was dismissive of the question – "That's nothing, boys. They carry away the Canteen waste like fruits and vegetable peels and the food wastes on the plates."

"Why do they take them away? I don't think they eat them."

"No, they rear cows, goats, poultry and pigs and take the waste to feed the animals. They had sought our permission and we had gladly granted because the canteen waste would be put to good use."

The two boys looked at each other and made eye signals. Justin said – "Okay Uncle, thank you so much for putting up with so many questions. Sorry to disturb you. Good night, Uncle."

There was a quizzical expression on Cyrus's face – "So, Holmes and Watson, are you going to solve this little problem for me?"

Tejas said – "We can always try, Uncle. But first we have to think."

Cyrus smilingly ruffled the hairs of the two kids – "Okay, Good night, then. But sleep with your thinking caps on."

Tejas and Justin came back to the dorm; the other three friends were eagerly waiting to know what happened in Cyrus Uncle's room.

Justin told them the details of the whole conversation that took place earlier. It seemed Cyrus Uncle also was concerned about the problem, but did not know how to get to the truth. The other boys just listened and nodded; they also did not have anything fresh to offer.

Tejas was sitting in one corner of the bed while Justin was narrating the conversation. He was trying to search his memory for something of vital importance, but it kept eluding him.

THE LITTLE JASOOS & OTHER STORIES

As the dorm lights were put off and the silence was all-pervading with the boys fast asleep, Tejas lay awake for a long time, still searching his memory.

After about a couple of hours, he suddenly sat up in bed and spoke loudly and spontaneously – "That's it! I got it!"

Justin was in the next bed; he was a light sleeper and was awakened by Tejas's utterance - "What happened, Tejas? What are you talking about?"

Tejas was calm now – "Not now, I shall tell you tomorrow morning."

Tejas Works It Out

More problems on the fifth morning – there was shortage of pears during the breakfast!

These pears were not the local variety, but the ones that grew in Kashmir and were called 'Babu Gosa'. They were not exactly cheap.

Kumar noted the problem, but remained clueless.

While coming out of the Canteen, Justin suddenly remembered Tejas's words in the dead of the night; he asked – "Tejas, what were you talking about in your sleep last night?"

Tejas shook his head slowly – "No, I was not talking in my sleep; I was fully awake. I found the clue to solve this mystery."

"What? You have solved the problem? Tell me, man!"

"Wait, you will see for yourself. If I am not mistaken, the mystery will be solved today itself."

Lunchtime threw up another shocking revelation – there was a shortage of paneer, another favourite item for most boys. The Canteen Supervisor Kumar could not hide his severe embarrassment, but had no clue about how this kind of phenomena kept repeating itself.

Tejas coolly told his friends – "Just wait till evening; such things will not happen again from tomorrow." He called Justin on the side and said – "Let's meet Cyrus Uncle immediately. We have to plan our action for later in the day."

Justin had no clue as to what Tejas was up to, but nodded and the two went in search of Cyrus Uncle.

Caught and Pardoned

At five O'clock, the football tournament matches started. Earlier, Tejas had requested the Sports Supervisor not to schedule any matches involving the five of them that day; they sat by the sideline and kept watching the match. But they had kept their eyes on the Canteen and the main gate.

At about six, after the dinner was cooked and kept ready, the kitchen helpers came out of the building and started walking towards the main gate to return to their village. Immediately, the five boys also got up and started walking in the same direction. But the surprising thing was – Cyrus also materialized from nowhere and stationed himself near the main gate along with the security guards.

Nothing unusual happened until the kitchen helpers reached the gate. Then the security guards stepped forward and asked those six helpers to leave the heavy carry bags in their hands near the gate and go home. Cyrus kept watching silently.

The helpers were at a loss – they had been carrying the kitchen waste every day for their animals and nobody had stopped them. Some conversation took place in Kannada between the guards and the helpers, but in the end, they left their load and walked out; they seemed to be somewhat shaken up.

With the help of the guards, the contents of the heavy carry bags were emptied on the ground. Hidden in the pile of peels and wastes were found about a dozen pears and six packets of paneer!

That night, Cyrus himself came to the dorm and congratulated the boys, Tejas in particular.

"I was joking with you last night, but truly you deserve to be called 'The Junior Holmes'. Looks like my 'Just Baby' is not a baby any more – henceforth I shall call him just 'Just'."

Rajesh promised to buy Tejas a Sherlock Holmes book after return to Nagarjuna, in recognition of his feat. Full of curiosity, he asked – "But Tejas, how did you guess that those fellows were pilfering the costly items that way?"

Tejas turned to Justin – "Just, do you remember I sat up in my bed last night uttering something?"

"Yes, but you did not tell me what made you do that."

"After coming back from Uncle's room last night and when you are telling our friends about what we talked there, I was trying very hard to remember something my *Dadu* told me long back; and then I remembered it very late in the night. I knew then I had found the answer."

Apurv asked – "What did your *Dadu* tell you?"

Tejas smiled and said – "He had told me a story long back about a similar incident taking place in his Kharagpur hostel during his student days."

Milind Cyrus was waiting in the dining hall the next morning with a big smile on his face. As the boys came for breakfast, he called them and said – "Those helpers are back for work today but have appealed for forgiveness. They said they were poor and were temporarily lured by the goodies of life."

Madhava asked in a surprised tone– "You are not going to punish them for what they did, Uncle?"

Cyrus smiled and said sadly – "If they don't work here, their families would starve. They are landless labourers and there is no agricultural activity in the summer. How will they earn money to feed their families? Temptations are vile things in life but even the richest fall for them. Anyway, they have realized their offence; I don't think they would do it again. Kumar will now keep a more watchful eye in the Canteen."

Before leaving for other areas in the campus, he said philosophically – "Being able to forgive makes you feel good inside; meting out punishment works the other way. That is a great lesson in life."

As he walked away with his head held high, the boys looked in his direction admiringly.

Lightning Source UK Ltd.
Milton Keynes UK
UKHW041231080219
336963UK00001B/246/P